RAVENS

THE HAWTHORNE UNIVERSITY WITCH SERIES
BOOK 5

A.L. HAWKE

PHANTOM HEART, LLC

ISBN: 9781953919625 (ebook)

ISBN: 9781953919595 (paperback)

ISBN: 9781953919465 (hardcover)

Library of Congress Control Number: 2024904413

Line edited by Stephanie Marshall Ward

Proofread by Alexa B., alexabooks.wixsite.com/authors

Cover © 2023 by Brosedesignz

Published by Phantom Heart, LLC

27702 Crown Valley Pkwy D-4, #201

Ladera Ranch, CA 92694, USA

Printed and bound in the United States of America

First printing March, 2024

Learn more about A.L. Hawke at www.alhawke.com

Correspondence: contact@alhawke.com

1

KNOCK, KNOCK, KNOCK

BRYCE AND I ARE SITTING TOGETHER AT A SMALL WOODEN kitchen table enjoying a nice quiet breakfast to celebrate our anniversary. It's our anniversary celebratory breakfast. Yeah, yesterday we had a wonderful quiet breakfast planned too, but it was interrupted by a bloody black raven with a broken wing fluttering on our porch, followed by a second knock heralding a young couple talking about their haunted house in White Hill, Missouri. Honestly, I prefer peace with my hubby. It gets my mind off all the things happening lately at Hawthorne University—like losing my soul.

I give Bryce a wink and raise my orange juice glass in a toast. The orange juice is really tart and yummy.

Then I gaze around our kitchen. I gotta tell you, my teacher, Alondra, had style. She installed Viking stoves, a marble island, and gorgeous travertine flooring. It's so lovely, like the rest of my house—or her house. Outside, through a small window, around all the thousands of trees of Hawthorne, it's a bit gloomy this morning. But it's warm and toasty indoors.

"What'cha thinking 'bout, babe?" Bryce asks, cutting sausage with a fork and knife.

"Nothing," I answer with a shrug.

There's a knock at the door—a third knock. He gets up.

"Forget it, Bryce. Let's just finish breakfast."

He nods and slowly sits back down.

"So, how was your visit with Kenosha?" he asks, forking some eggs. "You never told me. I spoke to her on the phone, but I haven't gotten to see her yet."

"I thought we weren't gonna talk about that stuff?"

"Just asking about Kenosha," he says with a shrug.

"But asking how Kenosha is doing is going to lead to talking about witchcraft. And talking about witchcraft is going to lead to discussing our coven. Talking about our coven is going to lead to your metaphysical class. And then, before you know it, professor, we're gonna talk about haunted houses, the couple yesterday, and White Hill, Missouri. And then—"

"Got it, Katie," he says with a laugh. "Forget it. So...what do we talk about then?"

"Nothing," I say with a shrug. "Absolutely nothing. That's what I really want to talk about, Bryce."

But we hear the knocking again.

"I mean, breakfast is our time to forget about our problems," I continue, ignoring the noise. I raise my orange juice glass again in a toast to him. "Happy anniversary, hun."

"Happy anniversary, babe."

But he still gets up.

He scoots his chair back and heads down our hallway. As we approach the foyer, under our crystal chandelier, something hits the door louder than ever. And it sounds a lot bigger than a bird. Bryce looks through the peep hole. He shrugs. Then he looks down.

"*Oh, my god!*"

He throws open the door.

"What is it, Bryce? Is it the bird again?"

No, it's not a small fluttering bird with a broken wing. Lying on the ground is a pale, naked woman shaking in a fetal position, bleeding from cuts all over her neck, chest, arms, and legs. There are so many cuts on her naked body that the dripping blood seems to have painted her skin red. She's weak and closing her eyes tightly. If her pretty blues opened, I'd recognize those infernal eyes. I already recognize her face: Enora. Yeah, Enora, my archenemy witch-bitch who tried to bleed me, kill my husband, turn my best friend insane, and cut Mira's throat has landed on our doorstep.

We stand over my archenemy in total shock, not doing anything. Then Bryce crouches down and lifts a blood-drenched wrist. Even her palm drips red over his hand and the sleeve of his navy blue robe. Under all that blood on her palm is the bitch's black backward pentagram.

"Bryce," Enora mutters weakly.

"Jesus, Enora, what happened to you?" I ask. But I keep my distance.

"Execrated."

"Help me take her inside, Cadence," Bryce says.

"No. No way."

"Cadence, she's hurt bad."

"So? Call 911. She can't come inside, Bryce."

"You want me to leave her by the door for dead?" he snaps, looking up. "Like the bird?"

"She probably was that bird, Bryce!"

"Come on, Cadence. Help me take her in."

"We'll just call 911, 'kay?"

"Cadence, help me bring her in," he says sternly, shaking his head.

"But why is she bleeding *everywhere*?" I ask. "There's deep red cuts and scratches all over. Was she whipped? Here's a better question, why the hell did she come here, Bryce?"

"She's wanted for murder," Bryce replies. "Kenosha threw her in jail for trying to kill Mira. Remember? She said *execrated.*

That means cursed. Maybe this was another spell by the Samhain Witch."

"Yeah, but...why did she come *here*? Does she want me to finish her off?"

"Cadence!" he says, shaking his head. "Enough. Help me bring her inside. She's not a dying bird."

"What if she dies inside the house? The cops might investigate and—"

He just looks up, still on his knee, staring right into my eyes.

"Fine. What do you want me to do?"

"Help me bring her into the guest bathroom."

He crouches down and grabs her by the shoulders. His hands slide along her skin because of all the blood. That's so gross. She's obviously unconscious. I think the slipping and sliding along her blood-drenched cuts would make her scream if she were awake. I reach down and pick up her feet. They're warm and slimy from all the fresh blood too. Then we carry her inside. I watch as all that blood drips over my lovely white marble floor.

"What are we going to do with her?" I ask.

"Clean her and dress her wounds."

"It looks like...*ew, gross!*"

"What!" he cries, backing up. Bryce nearly drops her. "What the hell is it now! What's the matter, Cadence?"

"Look at her leg, Bryce!" There's a piece of flesh dangling from her thigh surrounded by what looks like teeth marks. "I think something bit her!"

2

___

MY ANNUAL

"You can go inside now, Ms. Wallace."

About time. I've been sitting in this formal black suit in the hallway of the history department, shivering like crazy under the freezing forced air, for like an hour. It's really hot outside, but they're over-running the AC indoors. My suit is usually comfy, but it feels stifling.

As I walk into his office, the dean doesn't greet me.

Dr. Bainer is this short bald man with tanned skin and narrow glasses. He's sitting behind a large dark-mahogany desk. His office is a complete mess, with books and papers strewn all over his desk and bookshelves. Behind the messiness, through a large window, is a view of Hawthorne Forest under a cloudy sky. That's lovely. A couple kids with books under their arms walk by a bench under a bunch of trees. Between all those thick trees below are several lovely winding walkways. Hawthorne University is a beautiful campus, and at least I can look behind him and admire the nice view—not that he enjoys it. He probably never even noticed he has a view from his office.

But the weather is cloudy. It's getting stormy. Sometimes the heat mixed with wind and rain makes for perfect hurricane weather, and the possibility of one was forecasted on the radio this morning.

Dr. Bainer coughs.

I'm sitting with my legs crossed on a leather chair, with my black leather bag by my side, waiting.

And waiting...

He thumbs through printed reports I recognize—it's the files I submitted to the office last week. He looks annoyed. I kind of think I should be the one annoyed after waiting so long.

"I've been reviewing your dossier, Mrs. Wallace." He glances up, peering over his glasses. "I'd like to know why you didn't include a copy of your research paper? You should have a complete file for my review."

"It's not ready, professor. My preceptor was supposed to work with me, but she fell ill."

"Hmm," he grumbles, "people seem to fall ill a lot around you, don't they?"

Why you nasty little motherfucker.

But I force a smile. I already predicted this meeting was going to be a total disaster. "You know Dr. Trent is sick. She's my sponsor. She had a heart attack." He scoots the glasses up on his nose and nods. "She was supposed to review my work, and I was researching with her. Because she fell ill, I couldn't complete all your required papers."

He takes out another typed sheet and lifts it up over his head. I recognize it as my CV. He sort of examines it, scrutinizing every sentence for some reason. It's only a page. It's not very long, but maybe that's his fucking point?

"You included research on one topic," he says, picking up another sheet, "discussing the source of evil in the world. You even lectured about it, but I don't see any notes from Dr. Trent commenting on it. I think she would agree that the challenge will be connecting this philosophical argument to history. You're a graduate student in our history department, Cadence. I respect philosophical study, but your project will have to be grounded firmly in history. If you are to continue in our esteemed graduate program, you have to incorporate research in *history*; perhaps, if done properly, even postulate on things that have not been discussed before. Hawthorne University is a nationally renowned history college. The—"

"The metaphysical aspect of the class is the study of the mind," I argue. "One of the reasons, professor, this history college is so well known is because of Dr. Johansen's teaching here. I was trying to incorporate her philosophical subject into—"

"Philosophical study often has nothing to do with history. Dr. Johansen incorporated her subjects well. We tolerated her eccentric studies because it fit in with an appropriate history lesson plan for our students. So far, yours does not."

"This is just research. I haven't finished my proposal yet."

"Why haven't you submitted your proposal? Now that Dr. Trent is away, I could have reviewed your project in her stead. Can you at least tell me what you're planning?"

"Well…" I bite my lip. I really haven't thought much about it, to tell you the truth. Shh, don't tell. "I've been thinking about discussing the Inquisition."

"That's a rather broad topic."

"I was planning on tying accusations of witchcraft to the Templar knights. You know, the Knights Templar. When Dr. Johansen taught me, we had an assignment on them. I wanted to revisit that group and discuss the persecution of the knights and women in Europe over demonic practices, you know, maleficium, black magic and devil worship."

"I would suggest, then, Mrs. Wallace, that you move your topic a few centuries later, after the Knights Templar. As you know, most witchcraft persecution occurred in the 1600s, after the Black Death and Hundred Years War. In fact, white magic was still tolerated throughout much of Europe in the twelfth and thirteenth centuries. The Spanish Inquisition killed more Jews and Muslims than people accused of worshipping the devil. It relates more to racism than sexism. Your time period is not a good choice for a study of the witch trials."

"I know. But I told you I haven't worked it all out yet."

Then he just annoyingly nods...very slowly and methodically.

Fuck, I hate this guy!

"Did you like the rest of my stuff?"

He grumbles and starts thumbing through more papers he's already read a few times. I'm not sure I really want to know.

"Statement of Accomplishments," he reads, heaving a sigh. "Hmm. Two lectures. One on the subject of evil and the other on Joan of Arc."

"Joan of Arc is history."

"Yes, I was sitting in the audience for that lecture. I found your talk rudimentary. You were attempting to make it arcane."

This guy is *such an...asshole!* I mean, honestly! What the fuck is wrong with him?

"But I'm happy that you're lecturing. That is an accomplishment for any graduate student. Even though it's your husband's class."

I think I drank too much coffee. I'm so jumpy, my hands are twitching on the armrest of his leather chair. Or is it simply that I'm getting super pissed and I'm ready to leap up, flip him off, and run out of his office? I have a bit of a temper problem, you know. Last time he pissed me off like this I nearly launched a metal nail through his head.

I didn't like Raj much either.

Oh, hi Alondra. So nice of you to visit now. Mind telling me how the hell to get out of this disaster? It's kind of your fault being that you nearly killed the dean.

Raj isn't so bad, when you get to know him, Cadence. But you have more trouble to deal with right now than this interview, now that Enora showed up at your front door. Ask Raj how his daughter, Olivia, is doing in college in New Haven. Just throw a hint and your interview is over. Kenosha and her council of witches helped his daughter get into a university on the East Coast two years ago. She didn't have the best grades. She would never have made it in without Willow's help.

"Just shush, Alondra," I mutter. "Quiet, okay?"

"Excuse me?" Dr. Bainer looks up from the papers, amused. "What about Dr. Johansen? Why are you mentioning Alondra Johansen?" Then he chuckles. "You certainly can't get *her* to sponsor you."

"Sorry," I say, shaking my head. "Nothing."

Then he's back to rummaging the few papers in my file. There's really nothing there. I think I could have carefully read them two to three times in the time it's taken him to look them over. He keeps staring while sweat drips down my back—it's freezing in the hallway, but his office is hot, of course, like outside.

My cellphone buzzes in my black bag by my side. I take out my phone. Bryce texted:

I'm with Kenosha. Come here NOW.

"I have to go," I say, standing up.

"Hmm?" he asks, furrowing his brow and looking up. "What? We're not done, Mrs. Wallace. Where are you going?"

"Dr. Trent is sponsoring me, and she's back in town. She'll be back to work soon enough to work with me next year. Now it's getting really late. When you asked to meet, Dr. Bainer, you said ten, but it's nearly eleven. I just have to go. My review was supposed to be done by her, anyway, professor."

"Sit down, Mrs. Wallace. Dr. Trent might not be well enough to sponsor you for next year. You know, I had objections to you matriculating here for our graduate program. The provost went over my authority, and I was absolutely against her suggesting you work in your husband's class. I don't know how you two keep ending up working together in every class.

"There's a lot of odd things going on here on campus, including you living in Dr. Johansen's house and all the rumored goings-on in her backyard. Whether Dr. Trent comes back to work, *if* she comes back, I'm submitting my review to the committee regarding your status for next year. You might want to stay so I can go over that review with you. Perhaps we can work out a plan for you to be a better graduate student."

"Can't right now. Sorry, I really have to go."

He furrows his brow and folds his hands under his chin. Then he pompously shakes his head and points at my chair for me to sit back down.

"*If* you're still here next year, I'm going to suggest that you find a new sponsor—just make sure it's not your husband. As far as Dr. Trent, I disagree with a lot of her policies. It probably will be a better arrangement, anyway, if you use someone else."

"Well, Dr. Trent's not all bad, is she?" I ask. "I mean, she helped get your daughter, Olivia, into college despite her grades."

His skin turns pale as a ghost. And his mouth kind of opens like a fish.

"You asked to meet for my annual. I met. Now...blessed be... I mean, have a nice day, professor. Bye."

3

BREAD CRUMBS

I'm staring out a window on the second floor of the hospital with my hands in the pockets of my black slacks, waiting in Enora's hospital room. The wind is blowing the trees surrounding Hawthorne Hospital like crazy with some looking ready to keel over, snap, and be uprooted over my car. My slick dark-gray Jaguar is shaking so much in the storm it looks like it could flip over. This time, the weather is not wild because of my magic. I told you, they said on the news that we might get a hurricane or tornado. I didn't totally believe it when I was in Dr. Bainer's office. Now I do. It's turning dark as night and windy as hell.

I couldn't feel more awkward—actually, maybe I did at Dr. *Brainer's* office. Outside the hospital room sits a green-uniformed policeman in a bulletproof vest. Yeah, Enora's going back to the slammer. Not only that, but standing over my glassy-eyed archenemy in her blue hospital gown is this super weird man with a goatee. He is dark-skinned and tall with broad shoulders. He's wearing a black sports jacket and a top hat, and he is leaning on a cane. When I first came into the dark room, he was wearing sunglasses with one lens missing. He smiled at me, too, showing fangs. He has chiseled fangs as incisors. Apparently, like Gus, Enora's High Wizard last year, this guy chiseled his teeth into fangs to look like a vampire. Or maybe this one actually is a vampire? I don't know. This is the type of friends Enora surrounds herself with. Still, unlike her last man-slave, he looks like a gentleman. Or an undertaker.

The lights are off. That's not making it any darker, because thirty candles are lit around the hospital bed. It smells like incense: cinnamon and sandalwood. Those are Enora's favorite smells (along with sulfur). The hospital doesn't allow all this stuff. A nurse actually came in earlier and told them to douse the flames, but then the weirdo standing over her just took out a lighter and relit everything the moment she left.

On the nightstand I see a black wand leaning over a black book. The book has a bright red backward pentagram of course. Enora's grimoire? Probably. Only my witch-bitch arch-enemy could turn a sick visit in a hospital into a full-on witchy creep show. Wait. Actually, Bryce texted me to tell me he wheeled Kenosha to the cafeteria so that Kenosha could bargain with her witch friends in the witch council about Enora's fate. I suppose Enora's not the only weirdo here in Hawthorne.

"Funny how the wheel of life turns, eh, Katie," Enora says weakly. "I try to kill you and then end up on your doorstep needing your help."

I don't answer. I just look out the window.

"Then Willow fucks it all up by calling the cops to take me back to prison."

"You should have let me take you home, Panthera," says the weirdo standing over her.

"Amen, Aamon. Amen. I should have known little Katie would snitch after I sought her help. Of course, if she was her own witch by now, I wouldn't have been execrated on her hallowed ground. You really need to grow up, Cadence."

"You want to fight, Enora?" I snap, whirling back. "Is that why you showed up *at my doorstep*?"

Enora just laughs. But then she shuts up and gazes at the tray by her bed. They're giving her pain meds from a machine, and I think she's in a lot of pain. Her leg is bound up in gauze where the chunk of flesh was taken out, but her face, wrists, hands, and neck are still covered in scratch marks. Part of me is kind of glad about her pain. Sorry, but there's a wicked part of me that wishes all those cuts and scrapes had really injured her bad for doing everything she did to hurt me and my friends.

Light brightens up the room as the door is opened and Bryce wheels Kenosha inside in a wheelchair.

"Windstorm," Kenosha says weakly with a nod and grin. God, Kenosha looks so weak.

I return to my seat beside Enora. I've been trying to avoid the chair because it's too close to her bed.

"Had your meeting with your *council*, Willow?" asks Enora snidely.

"Yes, I did, Panthera. I told the triumvirate about your plight. The council is extremely worried about you."

"I don't give a fuck about them. Notice, Willow, I didn't come to your house, I came to my friend Katie's house. The council is worried about me? Perhaps they should be worried about themselves."

The man, apparently known as Aamon, nods and chuckles. Then he squints at Bryce. And then he turns those hypnotic icy-blue eyes on me. He's so weird.

"Dismiss your servant and we can talk," Kenosha says.

"I don't care for their decisions," Enora says, ignoring her order. Then she looks up at Aamon. "Aamon, can you be a dear and scoot me up a little. And then—" She yawns. "Talk to our guests. Won't you? I need rest. There's nothing for Kenosha and me to say to one another. We hate each other. I didn't come for her. I came for the Hawthorne Witch. For my dear friend Katie." The bitch chuckles. "I forgive your snitching, Windstorm. You weren't the one who called the police. But I have no interest in talking to this droopy, depressing willow tree."

"I called the cops too," I say.

Enora shakes her head and chuckles again.

"Panthera is in a lot of pain, witches," Aamon says. "Perhaps you all should come back tomorrow? Maybe, Willow, tell her more of your news and plans when she is feeling better?"

Although this man is doting on Enora, just like her last man-slave, Aamon sounds intelligent. Gus, Enora's last man-slave, was a complete idiot. And despite the fangs, Aamon has a strong jawbone and penetrating eyes. His eyes are so blue, like Enora's, even bluer in contrast to his dark skin. His beard is perfectly groomed. And he has a nice cologne. He'd be attractive if he weren't so fucking strange.

"Your servant needs to leave us," Kenosha says. "I repeat, dismiss him, Panthera. I will not discuss the council's decision in front of him."

"Actually, Aamon is a witch, Willow," Enora retorts. "I initiated him into my coven. He's my oungan."

"We know he's a witch, but he has no right in our affairs."

"Oh, but that's where you're wrong, he has every right in my affairs," she says, gesturing for him to lean close to her face. "Come."

She puckers her lips to his. At first, it's just a peck, but then they make out in front of us for an inappropriately long time.

"Can we get on with this?" snaps Bryce.

Enora unlocks her lips and smirks at Bryce. Then she winks at him.

Kenosha heaves a sigh in her wheelchair. "The headmaster

asks for you to join Windstorm and the Hawthorne coven in performing a shield spell."

"No," I snap. "No, my sisters won't ever work with Enora, Kenosha. They won't do that. None of our sisters will agree. Never."

"Cadence, let me finish," Kenosha says, lifting a finger. She shuts her eyes tightly for a moment. She seems so weak. It was probably all she could do to get her sister, Shirl, to bring her to the hospital. "Enora, a shield spell can be cast while Cadence officiates with her coven. No words from you will be permitted. We all know the traps set a few years ago by you and Bill Reardon. No traps this time, Cadence, if Enora isn't permitted to speak any incantations. Anyway, she'll be back in prison. Your Hawthorne coven will perform the spell. But you do need Enora, in spirit, to be present for her protection. The council can make arrangements for Enora to commune in spirit. I had planned on working on a shielding near Samhain again anyway, now I see the conjuring must be cast now. It will weaken the Samhain Witch. We already know that she wanders without a home but, apparently, your attack wasn't enough. Anyway, this is what you wanted, Enora. You went to Cadence's house and asked for help. She can cast protection every year now, like her teacher did."

"I'd rather Afreyea cast it," I object.

"She can't, Cadence," Kenosha says. "The violence is happening on your hallowed ground. You have to cast this shield spell. I can help... I live here now, but it has to be with your sisters in Hawthorne during our sabbaths. This town appears to be the Samhain Witch's main focus."

"Shield spells do shit, Willow," Enora says. "No. That bitch cut me good and chomped a hole in my leg. She's gonna pay. No, I'm not going to sit back and put some stupid trinkets around me for protection while whispering incantations in defense. I'm going to fucking kill—"

But she stops her tirade and closes her eyes for a moment. She seems to be in too much pain.

"Are you okay, master?" asks Aamon anxiously, kneeling and grabbing her hand.

"We need to kill her!" Aamon shouts, turning to us. "Our coven has already made the proper arrangements. You've tried for years to cast protection spells against this witch, Willow. You and Falconsong did. We need to either cast a spell to kill her or cut her throat. Either way, the only way is to take her life."

"The council does not condone murder," Kenosha says.

"And the council denies Satan worship," says Enora, forcing her eyes open again. "And the council denies organized occult practices. And you and your powerful friends never practice sex magic or involve yourself in worldly affairs, do you? Liar. Your witch council casts more evil than I could ever do."

"*Look at what that witch has done to her!*" shouts Aamon.

"Shh, Aamon," Enora says, patting his hand. "Shh. Calm yourself, dear. Just don't talk to her. I know how irksome and depressing Willow can be. Talk to Cadence. Talk to my dear friend Katie." She turns to me and forces a smirk. "Katie, even this hospital is on your hallowed ground. You made that clear enough to me last time, didn't you? The whole town is yours. Right? Well, look at what's happening to your town. Willow's in a wheelchair, Agnes is dead, and I was nearly eaten alive. I understand Kenosha wants to talk as *friends* and use amulets to protect us, but honestly, Katie, I don't think she or her council can do shit."

"Then who can, Enora?" asks Bryce.

"You," she says, smiling. "Well, not you, Bryce, I don't really see what you ever do. But your coven. Those retired witches Jane and Liam—maybe." Then she scoots back, staring at the ceiling. "*Maybe* Kenosha, if she'd stop consulting with her fickle, stupid, lame council."

"You would have had a better life if you had listened to some of those wise witches," Kenosha says.

"Well, neither you nor I are in any shape to argue right now, are we?" asks Enora. "We're really not in any shape to do anything. *Maybe*, Katie, think about it, *maybe* that's Melanie's point?"

"So the plan is to cast shield spells again?" I ask Kenosha.

I think that's stupid. I want to be angry about it, like Enora, but the last thing I want to do is agree with her and upset Kenosha more. Kenosha looks too sick.

"Yes," Kenosha says. "You and I will work together on a shield spell. Enora will commit her usual crimes in prison and probably continue to scry, watching you. The council knows that's what you've been up to all along, Enora."

"I don't think a shield spell will work," I say. "We have to stop Melanie."

"So you agree with us?" Aamon asks, surprised.

No, I don't think I'd ever agree with him. But I reply, "I only agree we have to do something—something different from what we've been doing."

"You've insisted that Alondra is inside of you, right, Katie?" Enora asks me. "Why do you think that is? I already told you. This monster is unfeeling. She isn't evil or good. She has become a force to simply hunt down and kill witches. No witch can shield us from her. The only one with that kind of power was our teacher, Alondra, and Agnes. They're both dead. You're really the only one who can help us, Cadence. You and I can kill Melanie with your witchcraft. I can't cast alone. But you and I could get rid of her for Hawthorne together."

"Can it be done in secret?" I ask.

"Cadence!" snaps Kenosha.

"Yes," Enora says with a smirk. "Yes, I think secrecy can be arranged. But her coveted council is far better with secrets than I am. Perhaps you should have Kenosha and her council friends help shroud your sins in the occult. They murder in secret so well."

"You said 'getting rid of her,' Enora," I say, shaking my head. "I mean…fighting her and stopping her using magic, I understand. But I don't want to kill her."

"You're not seriously considering attacking Melanie with magic again, Cadence?" asks Bryce. "After everything that happened?"

"If she did this to Enora, what's she going to do to you or me, Bryce?" I ask. "How is a shield spell going to keep her from committing violence? She has to be stopped. We even destroyed her home, and it did nothing."

"All those witches and Liam couldn't stop her, Cadence," says Bryce.

"But Enora wasn't with us."

"And what will she do to all your nice, happy friends?" Enora asks with a nod and an ungenuine smile. "Yes, yes, you're not as dumb as Willow, are you, Windstorm?"

"Only the darkest black magic can harm her, Cadence," Kenosha says, shaking her head. "Even if used against that beast, it's still a crime. Liam casted against her and it turned him. Agnes warned you about casting such evil before she died."

"*Fuck!*" Enora cries. I don't think she's upset with us; she's wincing in severe pain. "Fuck, that bitch hurt me, she hurt me real good! I tell you…while y'all go speak to your *councils*, cast shields, wear protective rocks, whisper prayers, rub your fingers over beads, or do whatever the fuck you all do, I tell you, my coven and I are going to hurt that bitch. Oh, I'm gonna hurt her real good. If any of you want to join me, wonderful. If not. Fuck off. Amen. Right, Aamon? Amen. Not atman. *My will be done.* Imprisoned by you or not, Willow, with Windstorm's help or not, I will find a way to cast vengeance. I swear it!" And she raises her left palm, tattooed with an upside-down pentagram. "Hail Satan."

Kenosha touches her chest. She closes her eyes tightly.

"Look at her, Cadence!" Enora rages, turning to me. "Look! Turn and look!" She grabs my hand and points at Kenosha. "Look over there! Look at Willow. Both of us were hurt, practically killed, by this witch! We're still suffering. This is not a time for crouching down with protective charms. We need to attack! I told you this a few months ago. This is your hallowed ground. You can stop this witch from destroying all of us if we fight. The only thing that monster cares about is destroying all practitioners of Hecate. That includes your husband, your friends, and everyone you care about. She will destroy everything, unless you help us. There's only one option."

She falls back, breathing heavily. Aamon falls on a knee again, with his head in his hands, by her side. He is covering his face and trembling as he crouches over her. Is he weeping?

I turn to Kenosha. She's sick, too, leaning over with her head in her hands.

"Do you hate me, Cadence?" Enora murmurs. "Don't trust me? I know. But this forces us to work together. We either destroy Melanie or she destroys us. Why do you think Alondra is inside you?"

"Show Cadence your arts, Raven," I say.

"What?" Enora asks, amused. "What did you say?"

But it's not just what I said, it's how I said it. I spoke in Alondra's voice.

"Alondra, why would you invite me to Hawthorne and then ask for Enora's help?" Kenosha asks. "Only dark magic can fight Melanie. And you asked for me to watch over Cadence and make sure she never goes down that path."

"But all the head witches are in peril," Alondra's voice says from my lips. "I see no other way."

Go away! Get out of my head! I don't want you inside me, Alon-

dra! Not just to talk about black magic, I don't want you speaking from my lips anymore!

"*Raven*, Cadence?" Enora chuckles in amusement. "*Raven?* So Alondra is inside you for real. You're not just losing your marbles."

"Let's go," I say, jumping up. Thank God it's my voice again. "I have to get away from her, Bryce. Yeah, you're absolutely right, I totally hate you, Enora. I can't stand another minute near you."

"Don't worry," Bryce says. "She won't be teaching you any black magic in jail."

"Oh really, Bryce?" asks Enora. "You think that? You want to know a little secret? Years back, when our mutual friend Mira was just a little girl, and you hadn't yet matriculated here at Hawthorne U., Alondra named her favorite of all the witches in her coven *Raven*. I lost the name under Selene when Bill and I submitted ourselves to the voice of Aiwass and enjoyed ceremonial fucking. I changed my name, under Lucifer, to Panthera. But I never lost the magic your teacher taught me. Nor did I forget the spell to change myself into my animal totem. Katie knew my bird. Amica. Remember, Katie? Amica means 'friend.' Cause we're friends, right?" The bitch laughs. She thinks that's very funny. "I did change you back to a human girl from a snake, but you tend to forget that I did you that favor. Anyway, amica, my raven form, is why no one can ever hold me behind bars, Bryce."

"I can see to it that there aren't any windows," Kenosha says.

"Melanie's smart, you know," Enora continues. "I blacked out. She must have attacked me when I was a little bird. It's far easier to maul someone and take a chunk out of their leg when they're under a foot tall." She turns to me. "So Alondra's inside you for real, huh Cadence? And she doesn't disagree with me about wanting to hurt Melanie? Like I said, ain't it interesting how the wheel turns? If it will help Hecate, sure, Alondra, I'll teach your favorite goody-goody pupil a thing or two. But there's gonna be a price. No witch here is turning the other cheek. I'm going to tear that fucking bitch limb from limb just as she did to my little birdie body. We don't turn the other cheek under the devil, do we, Aamon? We fight and slug back anybody who dares touch us." She raises her left hand, the one with the backward pentagram tattoo, closes her eyes, and says with a nod, "Hail Satan."

"Hail Satan," echoes Aamon with a nod.

"Help me go back home, Bryce," Kenosha says weakly. She's losing her color, and her hands are trembling.

"Sure," Bryce says. "Sure, Kenosha."

He turns her wheelchair. I walk with them to the door, and we don't even say goodbye, but I lurch back when I feel a hand on my shoulder. I spin around and see Aamon.

"Our coven needs protection," Aamon says. "Will you help us kill the Samhain Witch, High Priestess?"

"I'll... I'll do what I can to end this."

Kenosha doesn't pass out, but she doesn't say anything as we wheel her to the elevator. She keeps her eyes closed as we descend and head toward the hospital entrance. And I'm sure if she were strong, I'd have heard a mouthful by now about learning Enora's black magic. Bryce is quiet too.

When we approach the front of the hospital, Bryce says, "I'll drop off the wheelchair, Cadence, and take her home. I saw your parked car. I'll just meet you back home."

He stops the wheelchair in the waiting room by the entrance. Then he gently takes my arm and pulls me away from Kenosha.

"You can't have Enora show you magic. We spoke of all the stuff I did with Reardon. You know how much I've regretted that black magic. That wasn't Alondra. It's obvious Enora is just messing with your head."

"I know, Bryce. I can't stand her. But I don't want to talk about it right now. I really don't like either plan, shield spells or black magic. I just need to think it over. Something has to be done for the town."

"Okay." He leans over and kisses my cheek. "Love you, babe. Be careful out there. They say the eye of the storm passed, but it's still really bad outside."

4

CHOCOLATE ICE CREAM

I'M SITTING IN A BOOTH IN AN ICE CREAM PARLOR ABOUT A BLOCK from the university. It's called Hawthorne Sweets and I absolutely love it. All the walls are windowed, and the counter reflects the painted peach and pink walls. Behind the counter, workers make these colorful confectionery masterpieces. There are even two huge statues of triple scoop ice cream cones by the entrance.

Outside my large window, I catch groups of students, wearing backpacks, walking together down a one-lane road amid the trees. This ice cream joint isn't far from university housing; in fact, Kenosha lives right down the block. It's warm, so all the students are in summer clothes. But, despite the clear skies, so many trees shadow the road that the path seems dark.

When I was a student, Maddie and I used to go to this parlor right before finals. It was one of our private traditions, a break before more studying. It's a quaint little downtown ice cream parlor with large peach vinyl booths and a classic diner look, where you can stare outside while spooning your favorite goo. You can get classic ice cream floats and shakes, but I always go for the stacked sundaes. The only disadvantage is the effect on one's waistline, you know. But with all the shit going on right now, I'm not sure I care.

A waitress in an old-fashioned peach apron comes over to our table with two large metal bowls of triple scooped chocolate and strawberry ice cream sundaes coated with malt candy, chocolate chips, and whipped cream smothered in hot fudge and covered with a handful of cherries. Complete bliss, I tell you.

Frida sits across from me in the booth. Poor Frida has been acting depressed as hell and hasn't spoken to any of us in weeks. She hasn't said much since we sat down either, but she smiles at the huge sundae before her.

I lift up a spoon and click the iced silver bowl. "Bon appétit," I say.

"Why'd you want to meet here, Katie?" Frida asks with a chuckle.

"Because I love it, Frida," I say, spooning some bliss. "This ice cream here is to die for."

"You're funny, Katie." And she laughs.

And that smile is genuine and so sweet.

"Sure, Frida. Sure."

I take another spoonful of luscious chocolate ice cream and mix it with hot fudge. Then I spoon more in my mouth. I say, "Frida, our sisters in the circle have been worried about you. You missed our last couple ceremonies. Not only that, I haven't even seen you in church. You're not answering your phone. This year's tough enough, you know. Bryce and I are doing every-thing we can to make Alondra's class great. And there's not a lot of time left for us to be together, particularly you and me. You know, once you and Greg tie the knot and when you guys head back to New York, I won't be seeing you."

"I know, Katie."

"Yeah, I guess." I pause and scoop a chocolate chip dipped in fudge. I swirl it around the pink ice cream. It's so good!

"Many of our sisters have been hurt that you haven't answered your phone."

She shrugs. Then she turns to the window and stares at the kids walking along the street. It's then that I realize Frida's not wearing any witchy makeup. But then I realize, with far more shock, that she hasn't touched her sundae.

"Your friendship means a lot to me, Frida."

"I'm leaving next month," she says with a nod, staring out at the trees. "I've had a great time at Hawthorne. But yes, Katie, Greg has a job in New York. So we won't be seeing each other much after that, I'm thinking."

I put my spoon down.

"Frida, what the hell's the matter? You've just disappeared. Whether you're leaving or not, you're in front of me now."

"Nothing," she says, shaking her head and frowning.

"Are you going to eat your sundae?"

Then, typical of my sweet friend, she spoons some ice cream mixed with whipped cream and chocolate chips—just because I asked her to. She doesn't look like she wants to.

"It's really good, right?"

"It's very good, Katie," she says with a nod. Then she looks out the window. "But I always preferred vanilla."

"You could have gotten vanilla."

"No. No. It's fine. You told me how good this sundae is."

It sure is. I take another spoonful.

"Can you come this Friday?" I ask with my mouth full. "Everyone's asking about you. Your best friend, Helen, says she misses you so much in ceremony. And even my brother says it's not the same without you—even though you know how I feel about it when he shows up. You know, I'd much rather you be there than him."

She nods and tries to smile.

"Frida...what the hell is it?"

She pauses and takes a deep breath. "Katie, I'm upset about Agnes." And she almost comes to tears.

"Agnes? That was a couple months ago."

But I don't think that makes her feel any better. I don't get it. The sweet old woman died. So? I mean, I feel bad about it, but I've moved on. Why is she still so disturbed by it? She's acting like Agnes was her grandmother or something.

"Frida..."

But I don't say anything else. Instead, I twirl my spoon in the ice cream. Then I feel guilty. This is not going to do my figure any good. I haven't found the time to exercise lately, you know. Why is it that the most amazing pleasures in life are full of guilt? The things I sacrifice for my friends.

"We were all shocked about what happened," I finally say with a shrug.

She shakes her head. But then she nods.

"I just need time, Katie," she says. "I'm sorry. That woman was so sweet, one of the nicest and sweetest old ladies I've ever met. She was so nice to me in the house before she died. I can't believe that happened to her, of all people. It just seems that every year something horrible happens to us. Remember Reardon? And Enora? Remember what Enora did to Reardon in front of us?"

Yeah, she stabbed him to death in front of us. That memory kind of makes me not want to eat any more ice cream.

Nope...too good.

I reach for her hand, but she jerks it away.

"And you, remember what happened to you when you were a snake?" Frida shakes her head vehemently. "I need a break, Katie. I just need a break from it all."

"You're not the only one who's having a hard time."

"I know," she says, finally taking my hand. She smiles. "I know. You're having it so much harder than any of us. But that doesn't make it any better for me."

"But church? Why haven't you come to church, Frida? You got me to go there in the first place. I get that you want a break from the coven, but why aren't you coming to church?"

"I love that you're going. I told you, I just need some time."

How much more time does she need? We don't have any more time. She's leaving.

A girl with dark hair, dark gothic makeup, a gray T-shirt, and a skirt walks right by our window carrying three books under her arm. I squint. Among the student's textbooks, I recognize one published by Alondra. Alondra published a handful of books, and Bryce uses some of them in class. That one is a bit more esoteric, on the subject of sigils. Hmm. I'll have to keep an eye on this student. I need new recruits next year. She certainly looks gothic enough to want to check out our circle.

I look back at Frida. She's just twirling her spoon in her ice cream bowl. I notice for the first time that her nails are polished soft pink.

Her eyes are watery.

"Oh, Frida."

"Hmm?" she asks, blinking hard and forcing a smile.

5

SPRING FESTIVAL

I'm staring at two huge bonfires, amid the wild grass, where a thousand kids have gathered to celebrate the season. More people are here in the backyard of the Billington house than in the entire town of Hawthorne tonight. Of course, there's no Billington house. Turning to my left, away from all these crowds, and squinting through darkness, I can just make out a huge ditch. Only one short wall stands. The rest of the Billington mansion—except the basement—has been completely destroyed. It was just last year that Enora's minions burned down the historic three-story Billington mansion (another reason I hate that witch).

But I love Beltane.

Everyone is laughing and smiling tonight, loving the festival. Honestly, I wasn't sure I'd make it because of all of this year's craziness. I've missed so many Beltanes at Hawthorne, and we have one of the biggest ceremonies in the country, maybe the world. The weather was awful last week, but it's clear skies and a perfect warm evening for the celebration.

I'm standing with Madison, Aunt Jane, and my hubby near a large group of spectators. My friends and I are wearing our black cloaks—except Aunt Jane. Aunt Jane is just wearing this pretty long green dress. And we've all got white flower garlands in our hair. Our group, among many more spectators, forms two long rows in a clearing in the woods that ends beside two large bonfires. Ladies in white dresses have already passed through the center, along with bohemian flute players in bird masks and men painted red holding drums and tambourines. Other men, painted green, are doing gymnastics, jumping, and twirling past us. Many of the boys are half-naked, wearing only underwear, with their faces and bodies painted. Some girls are also wearing only underwear with their boobs painted red. Looking closely through all the makeup, I don't recognize any of these faces from school. I think the ceremony is so popular that it brings people from all over the country. Most of the revelers look intoxicated. I've had a beer and a half myself, so I feel pretty good right now.

Aunt Jane laughs and points at adorable little boys wearing white suits accompanied by small girls in white dresses holding flowers. They remind me of flower boys and girls at weddings. They're so cute.

Seeing Maddie's mom here is weird. She was so angry when I ratted Maddie out about going to Beltane when we were freshman. Now she's volunteering to be with us? Hmm, how the wheel of life turns, as that bitch Enora pointed out.

A little farther down the aisle, I see my brother, Damie, and Dad. Damie's wearing a black cloak too. Dad is the only "normal" guy, wearing a button-down and slacks, but seeing him feels weirder than standing beside Aunt Jane. The rest of my gang is mixed in with the crowds. But if I squint hard enough, I catch more of our sisters in black Druid cloaks.

"Aunt Jane?"

"Hmm? Yeah, Cadence?" She's still staring, with a big grin, at all the cute little kids walking by us.

"I saw Enora."

"That witch who attacked Madison?" Jane asks, losing her smile.

"Same one, Mom," Maddie interjects beside me. "Oh, look, Cadence! Never mind that wicked witch. It's Tammy! She came! She came! She's all dressed like the May Queen again!"

And her arrival is heralded by the sound of more drums and flutes, blaring like crazy, in the audience. I'm squinting, but I can't spot her yet. I need glasses now, okay? Tammy was the May Queen last time I saw this festival, when I was a freshman. She must have come all the way from Savannah just to perform.

There she is! Around a bunch of crazy men, painted red, hammering large drums and dancing around her. Tammy's bald head is covered with a huge flower garland. She's slowly walking down the aisle in a lovely draping white dress, contrasting with her dark skin. And her face has a red line over her eyes and is covered with white powder. But it's our Tamms for sure.

"Hi, Tammy!" cries Maddie as she walks by.

"Oh, hi Cadence," she says excitedly, waving to us. "Hi guys!"

When Tammy approaches the two huge bonfires, all the guys by the fire go crazier, dancing around her. Two men in dark Druid outfits, not much unlike the ones we wear, direct Tammy to stand between the towering flames. Then more men jump and do somersaults around her. A few men even jump through fire. Another passes in front of Tammy doing handstands.

"I wish Kenosha were well enough to see this," Bryce says to me. He sips some beer from a red cup. I sip mine. Then he squeezes my free hand. "It's amazing, Cadence."

"Yeah, Bryce. It's really cool."

"Where'd you see that wicked witch?" Aunt Jane asks me. But with all the flutes and drums, I hardly hear her.

"She showed up on our doorstep," Bryce hollers. "Then we saw her in the hospital."

"That horrible witch is sick?" Jane asks. "Good. But she came to your house?"

I nod.

"Katie, this isn't a good time," Maddie says, leaning close to my ear.

Yeah, but...whenever is a good time?

"Enora wants Cadence to help cast magic against the Samhain Witch," Bryce says, leaning toward Jane. "She thinks that she needs to teach her dark magic to hurt her."

Flutes and whistles blare to my left. Then a man painted from head to toe in green passes by. He has a large black top hat, a lot like the hat Enora's High Priest was wearing in the hospital, and he's twirling a cane. Green paint covers his shirtless chest, under a black sports jacket. His dancing really excites the crowd. The last time I saw the ceremony, Bill Reardon played the Green Man. Reardon was such an old fart that he barely moved, but this guy is moving like a pro. He has a goatee, like Aamon. Wait... Oh, my god, wait a second! This guy doesn't just *look like Aamon, he is Aamon!*

I turn to Bryce. Bryce nods with eyes wide.

"What is it, guys?" asks Maddie.

"What did that evil witch want?" shouts Jane. "I didn't hear you, Bryce?"

"She wanted to teach Cadence magic to hurt Melanie," Maddie shouts to her mom.

Both Bryce and I don't say anything. Our mouths are gaping as we stare at the Green Man.

"What the hell's the matter, guys?" asks Maddie.

"That man playing the Green Man was in the hospital with Enora, Maddie," Bryce says, pointing at him. "That's Enora's new High Priest."

"Him? Are you sure?" asks Maddie. "Really? I heard they found someone from Atlanta at the last minute. But, so? Didn't they discharge Enora and send her back to jail?"

Yeah, but Enora was hurt bad. Why would this guy, who seemed to care about her more than anything in the world, just drop everything, abandoning the wicked witch he cared so much about, all to perform in a play? I mean, I get how important the Beltane ceremony is, but it's weird. Especially considering how worried he seemed in the hospital.

He doesn't seem upset now. He and Tammy stand together between the flames as fire dancers continue to jump around them, doing more handstands and somersaults. Then Aamon dances around Tammy, doing a better job with his moves than the men painted red. Maybe performing is Aamon's job? He's certainly an amazing dancer.

Finally the movements stop and Tammy and Aamon embrace and kiss passionately. Then men in black cloaks, like our witch robes, walk up and tie their hands together to complete a fake handfasting, or pagan wedding.

We all clap like crazy. They're ceremonially married, and the Beltane ceremony is over.

"We should probably wait for the crowds to die down," Aunt Jane says. "Thanks for inviting me, Bryce." Then she waves. "Rick! Hey, Rick, will you come over here? How did that man get so far away from me again? Your dad can get so absent-minded sometimes, Cadence."

"Damie!" cries Maddie. "Hey, Damie, get down here! Cadence, your family really needs to wake up. What's the matter with you guys?"

"We love them," Bryce says, giving me a hug. He kisses my cheek. "Happy Beltane, Cadence."

"Happy Beltane, Bryce."

Jane taps my shoulder from behind.

"Cadence, Liam and I went through all this with you," Jane says. "Your dark magic incantation was used to free Liam. That was all. Under no circumstances should you *study* dark magic. Any magic that evil witch could teach you is evil. You mustn't ever do it. Okay?"

Sure. But as all our friends rush over, there's no time to tell Jane that Alondra was asking Enora to teach me.

Our whole gang approaches a bunch of open white tents beside the fields. It's still busy and kids and adults are dropping off costumes or taking off makeup. Bryce spots Tammy in one of the main tents, holding a large white sponge before a mirror, and we run over. A bunch of men are beside her, washing off their red makeup beside her chair. One lady is removing the red makeup from her face. (I hope she chooses a bathroom to remove the paint from her chest.)

"Hey guys!" Tammy jumps up from a stool and embraces me. "I've missed you so much."

"We've missed you so much, you don't even know," I say.

"Hey, Tamms!" cries Maddie, hugging her.

"Where are you staying?" I ask.

"I got a hotel in town."

"Next time, stay at our place," Bryce says.

"I heard from Mira about all the craziness you and the coven have been dealing with," says Tammy, shaking her head. "And I heard of the death of a witch and Kenosha getting hurt. I didn't want to trouble you guys with everything going on."

"Whatever's going on, you're always welcome," Bryce says.

"I'm just happy to have been invited again to play the May Queen. It's so much fun. The fraternity almost didn't have it here this year."

"They delayed the rebuilding just for the ceremony," Bryce says.

"So I heard," Tammy says.

"And here's Mom." Maddie is bringing Aunt Jane and my dad over.

"Hey, Tammy," Jane says.

"Hi, Aunt Jane!" Tammy hugs her. "Hi Maddie. It's so good to see all you guys. You all look great!"

"You performed wonderfully, Tammy," Aunt Jane says.

"Tammy, this is my dad," I say.

"Mr. Hawthorne?" Tammy asks with a big grin. "Really? You're Katie's dad? It's so nice to finally meet you!"

"It was a magnificent play," Dad says, reaching out a hand to shake.

Tammy just throws her arms around him. "Happy Beltane, Mr. Hawthorne."

"Hmm," Maddie says right by my ear. "How 'bout that, Cadence? Ain't it interesting how Mom and your dad are showing up together so often these days?"

Bitch. I get the hint. Why doesn't she just come out and say it?

"What are you doing tomorrow, Tammy?" Bryce asks. "You want to come over for dinner? Or lunch?"

"Sure, I'll still be in Hawthorne. Nate's flying me back Monday. He's off to Los Angeles, and then he'll be zooming back and picking me up by rental car. Then we're driving home."

"There's still a keg by the pole here, guys!" interrupts a guy in a dark cloak at the tent entrance. He looks so drunk that he could collapse the tent. We all laugh, but when he spots Bryce, *Professor Wallace*, beside me, he loses his smile and makes a hasty exit.

"Tammy," Bryce says, turning back, "do you know the guy who played the Green Man?"

"No." She is furrowing her brow. "He was some actor they pulled at the last minute." She laughs. "I kept wondering who I'd be marrying this time."

"Is he still here?" Bryce asks. "We'd love to talk to him and congratulate him too."

Sure would. How creepy. But Tammy just shrugs.

6

———

THE SCARLET LETTER

"HERE, GUYS," MADDIE SAYS, HANDING ME AND TAMMY LARGE margarita glasses full of some blended green ice cocktail. I'm leaning against a wood column on the patio entertaining my favorite guest. I heave a sigh. It's just such a perfect night for an outdoor barbeque.

Tammy sips it. "You make this, Maddie? Yum. It's really good."

"What is it?" I ask. It tastes icy and fruity.

"Lime margaritas."

"It's super good," Tammy says, nodding. "Show me the recipe, will you?"

"Easiest recipe ever, Tamms. Mash up ice in a plastic bag, pour the contents of the bag over the frosty blend from your nearest Hawthorne market, and there you have it."

"It's a mix?" I ask with a laugh.

"Yeah," Maddie laughs and touches my shoulder. "Great, right? Your brother's the bartender this evening."

"Tell him it's great," Tammy says with a laugh.

"Hey, Damie!" Maddie shouts toward the sliding door, which is slightly ajar. "Damie, can you make another one for

Bryce?" She turns back to us. "Bryce is so busy flipping burgers that he hasn't had anything yet."

Then Maddie walks through the sliding glass doors into our living room. "Did you hear me, Damien? Do me a favor and—"

The sliding door shuts.

I look up at the sky again. Tammy does too. The night sky above is so clear, and all the stars are sharp. Tonight it's warm and perfect.

Bryce, Natasha, Mandy, Josie, and Debra are hanging around the barbeque. Shy Helen—who's bald like my good friend Tamms here, but has kind of the opposite disposition—is sitting at an outdoor table alone, reading a book by candlelight. Helen might be shy, but she's not that shy around us. She's simply comfortable quietly studying alone tonight. We all feel comfortable together, of course. I spot Jessica and Chandra, our other two shy witches, strolling along the outskirts of my glade. This is our coven. We might be witches in ceremony, but we all love each other as close friends.

The bright moon casts the shadows of the surrounding trees onto the wild grass. I take a deep breath enjoying all this fresh woodsy air—and the smell of burgers from my hubby's barbeque.

"Have you seen Frida?" Tammy asks.

"Hmm?" I ask. "No. I met with her for ice cream at Hawthorne Sweets. Everyone's been wondering what the hell happened to her. She's so freaked out about Agnes's death..."

"I heard that," Tammy says, losing her smile. "Sorry, Cadence, but I'm kinda glad I wasn't here when it happened."

"I'm glad you weren't here too. It was horrible. But it's weird that she didn't come tonight to the party. She said she'd make it to Beltane. I didn't see her in church again this morning either." I turn to Helen. "Hey Helen, have you seen Frida around?"

Helen furrows her brow and shakes her head, but she's still staring at the textbook she's reading. She just shrugs.

"Frida hasn't been herself," Tammy says. "She's been acting so fearful on the phone. I think that creeped me out more than Mira's stories about what happened in Alabama. I've been worrying about all of you. But..." She smiles a rueful grin. " Particularly you, Cadence. Frida's worried a lot about you too." She sips some of her margarita. "Do you still have...you know... is she still *inside you?*"

She doesn't really sound like she wants to know.

"I wish she weren't."

"But is it really her, Cadence? Alondra?"

Then Tammy does something I hate, which everybody's been doing for the past few months. She studies my eyes. I cover my eyes with my free hand.

"Stop, Tammy. I hate my eyes."

"*Your* eyes are fine. Just not *Alondra's.* Cadence, if she's really in there, can you tell her—"

"No. Absolutely not, Tammy. I won't tell her anything." I really don't mean to be rude. I love Tammy so much, but every time I tell someone who knew Alondra that her spirit is inside me, I suddenly become some weird medium asked to send a long-lost message to Alondra that wasn't unveiled before she died. "No way. No. I don't want her to come out."

"Fine," she says with a chuckle. "Jeesh, if you're that defensive, I believe you. But it's absolutely incredible." She sips more of her margarita.

"What's the story with you and Nate?" I ask. "Aren't you guys—"

"Shh." Tammy leads me by the elbow a little farther away from Helen. Helen's so engrossed in her book that she doesn't seem to notice. She whispers, "Be real quiet 'bout this, cause the plans aren't set in stone. But, Katie—" She reveals a big smile. "We're going to get married. He showed me a ring." Then she puts a finger over her lips, staring at Helen.

"Oh, Tamms," I say softly, "Tamms, I'm so happy for you."

"I know. I know. Not too unexpected, right? We just have to get all the arrangements together. It's probably going to be a destination wedding. I mean, he's a pilot."

"I'm so happy for you."

Helen looks up. She looks right at Tammy and grins. Did she hear? No way. We were so quiet. But did she *feel* it? All of my witches have various unique talents. Helen's is clairvoyance. She's probably a better fortune teller than I am. Maybe that's why she's so shy?

"Jamaica?" Helen asks Tammy with a big smile.

"Helen, stop spoiling all my surprises!" Tammy snaps.

"Is she right?" I ask with a laugh.

"Helen's always right, Windstorm," Tammy says. "You know that."

"Congrats, Tammy," I exclaim. "I expect an invite soon."

"Don't be telling the High Priestess the date yet, 'kay, Helen?" Tammy teases.

Helen puts a finger over her lips. Then she jumps up, rushes over to Tammy, and hugs her.

"Hey, sis," Damie says. He is walking outside carrying another margarita in one hand and an envelope in another. "I found this by the front entryway table. It's for you."

I snatch the letter.

Damie walks over to Bryce and hands him a margarita. Then Maddie comes outside. After Helen breaks the news, she and Tammy start going crazy. The letter is from the university. That's weird. I tear open the envelope.

Dear Cadence Wallace,

I regret to inform you of your dismissal from the doctoral program in history at Hawthorne University. After reviewing your performance this year, your proposed topic of study, your research paper draft, and your grades here at the university, the graduate program committee has decided not to approve you for further study next year.

This decision was a difficult one. It is based on your performance and your lack of progress towards what we have come to expect in our esteemed program. As you know, Hawthorne University is world renowned in historical studies.

You have a right to appeal. This decision can be reversed if you properly remediate grades in the classes listed on the following page AND if you choose a professor to represent you this summer who can help you better plan your research proposal (said professor cannot be an assistant professor or, for obvious nepotistic reasons, Dr. Wallace).

Sincerely,

Dr. Rajan K. Bainer

Distinguished Professor of Historical and Anthropological Studies, Hawthorne University, Hawthorne, GA

Fuck.

Tammy and Maddie are still laughing with Helen. They're all talking about weddings now. I feel like I was just hit over the head by a baseball bat.

"Did you hear, Cadence?" Maddie asks.

Fuck.

I nod, staring back down at my letter.

"Cadence?" Maddie repeats. She walks closer. "Cadence, did you hear?" She furrows her brow. "What's wrong?"

Madison is reading my mind again. But I don't want her to read my mind this time. I don't want to tell anybody about this. For the first time ever, after thinking about Helen, I wonder if clairvoyance is Maddie's secret witch power. I always thought it was just that we love each other, but she always *feels* when there's something wrong with me.

"I gotta go to the little girl's room, Maddie," I say. "Sorry, I'll be right back."

I quickly make my exit.

I hear Josie in the kitchen cleaning the blender. Everyone else is outside.

I make my way upstairs, in the dark, to my bedroom. I sit down on my bed and stare outside through our floor-to-ceiling window facing the backyard. I can see the light of the fire from the barbeque below and all my friends hanging out enjoying themselves in our forest glade. Surrounding them are the shadows from all the trees of the forest. Otherwise, it's dark.

I look down at the letter in my hands. God, what am I going to tell Bryce? Dr. Bainer hates me so much. This man hates me more than anyone, I think, has ever hated me in my life. Maybe even more than Enora.

I glance down at the letter again. I'm such a complete idiot. He obviously set up that interview not just as an annual review, but as an excuse to talk to the graduate committee about expelling me. He's wanted me gone from the beginning of the year. But it's so unfair. I wasn't ready for my review because I was working with Kenosha. I knew Kenosha would be back and let me pass no matter what I prepared for my final review. I knew all those lectures would mean something to the provost. It's funny because I always thought Kenosha was the bad guy.

I stand up, stretch, and take a deep breath. Then I turn and look at the head of the bed. For a moment, I remember my teacher lying there. Those last horrible weeks when she was dying. Back then, Alondra spent all her time in this bed. I'm not in a trance. I guess the horrible news is reminding me of her suffering.

"I'm sorry, Alondra," I say quietly. "I'm so sorry to disappoint you. I messed up real bad this time."

She doesn't answer. I think it's because I really don't want her to appear right now. But I know she would be just as disappointed in me as I am. Then I think of Dr. Bainer. I hate him so much. Part of me wants to hurt him. I could. I'm a witch. I could curse him. I could hurt him just like he's hurting me right now.

I crumble the letter tightly in my fist. I crumble the paper so hard that I feel my long fingernails and the folds of the paper cut my skin. I squeeze until I feel a sharp pain in my palm, and that pain makes me squeeze even harder. Then it feels sticky. Is that my blood?

I make my way back down the stairs to the living room, and I have to heave the sliding door hard to open it. It always jams. All my friends are near the barbeque now except Maddie. Maddie waited for me, standing on the patio.

"What's wrong, Cadence?" Maddie asks again. "What's the matter?"

"Nothing."

When I look at the door, I see red dripping down the metal handle. My palm is trailing blood.

I rush over to our outside trash can and throw the letter away. Then I grab a paper towel from the patio table and cover my bloody hand.

Maddie's staring at me.

"I'm fine, Maddie," I snap. "Okay? Stop it. Forget it."

"Sure, Kates," she says, touching my shoulder and forcing a smile. "Sure. Just tell me later. Anyway, everyone's going crazy right now over Tammy's news. Natasha and Mandy are building our fire. Come with me to the fire, High Priestess, so you can join us and congratulate her."

7

A DARK MANNER

Up a green, grassy hill, toward a large one-story white manor, I feel the soft blades of grass brush along my bare feet. Those grass needles feel pleasant over my skin. So does the sun, warming my face and body. I touch my hips and belly. I'm naked. I don't know where I've placed my clothes. I don't care. My confidence makes me think this is a witch wandering...but, how? This isn't Hawthorne.

Cocking my head back, I see a small cemetery, and beyond that is a one-lane road, and beyond that, a lovely large dark lake. This isn't the small lake on campus, where I can see shore to shore. At the top of the grassy knoll is a one-story white house with cottage windows.

I come to the house and peek through a glass window. It's dark inside. Yellow light flickers along the white plaster walls of intersecting hallways, probably candlelight, but it's hard to see.

A door is ajar.

Inside it's dark and cold. The coldness is strange after being outside beside the sunny loch—*loch*, yes, that's what that lake is. It's not a lake; in these parts, it's known as a *loch*.

The flickering light brightens as I pass a room, midway

down the corridor, where dishes are stacked on a counter by a sink. The tile floor is cracked and dirty here. Some of the walls are blackened and charred. And a burnt and broken wooden chair is leaning against a wall. The kitchen? It's in ruins.

I continue down the hall and enter a larger room. I'm not alone. In the center of the room, in a large red circle, three women and two men are standing perfectly still, like statues. They are wearing dark cloaks and holding lit black candles to their chests. Under the cloaks they are naked. Black domino masks cover their eyes, disguising their identity. Inside the circle, a red line connects their positions, forming a five-pointed star. They're facing an empty raised wooden chair sitting to my right. Draped behind the chair is a long black cloth with a large red backward pentagram. Wooden and metal crosses and a large gold chalice are leaning on a table opposite a fireplace. And other shapes—six-, seven-, even eight-pointed stars—are hand drawn all over the wooden chair and cloth. There's also a large skull with horns on the table.

I hear the soft beating of drums. Very soft, almost inaudible, in a steady hypnotic rhythm. It's pleasant.

"Come forth, lovely virgin soul. Come forth with thy sacrifice."

The words are said by a dark-skinned man, in an Egyptian headdress and bull mask entering the room. He has a long, ornate gown and a leopard skin draped over his shoulder. With a wave of a long black wand, he gestures for me to sit at the altar. I hesitate. But then the three women leave their circle and approach me. One reaches for my hand and leads me gently to the raised dais.

I sit.

The man in the bull mask steps closer, waving his wand a few more times before me. Then he turns his back to me and removes his Egyptian headdress. He is bald. He drops his robe, revealing his bare back and ass.

"Upon our gods, do what you will, brothers. Sisters. Do whatever you want."

"We do as we will," they all echo in chorus. "We do whatever we desire, brother."

"Amen," whispers a voice in the darkness. "Amen."

"In trance lucidity, we ask the sacrifice to forfeit inhibitions. We ask her to offer herself as sacrifice for the energy of this order." He bows, still with his back to me, holding his headdress in his hands. "Baptized under Baal, upon blissful sexual lucidity, we sacrifice a life force, for the benefit of Baphomet, in magic. Not magic with a 'c,' brothers and sisters, *magick* with a 'k.'"

"Amen," they all say.

"Baal," they all say in unison, with a nod, glancing at me.

"Baal. Baal. Baal."

A lady with long dark hair walks to my chair and grabs the gold chalice. "Drink," she says, lifting the cup to my lips. She smiles. "Drink."

I shake my head.

"Drink and you shall be reborn," she says excitedly. "No longer of this body. You shall take another. Shapeless. Devoid of mystery. Like blessed Choronzon, vying to be seen. Made visible upon all other gods of the occult. A brighter light than night. Plainer than day. You've already tasted from the cup. Drink again and be reborn from your dream by ceremony."

I shake my head again.

A blond woman with that same domino mask approaches. Together they hold the chalice under me.

"Drink," she says with a smile and a nod.

"Drink," a third girl, with short dark hair, says. She shakes her head and smiles. "Drink and there is no hesitation. Drink and you will be free to do whatever you wish, baptized under the true savior of our world. You."

This girl comes close to my face. Too close. Her small black eye mask grazes my cheek. Then she gently touches her soft lips to mine. The other girls explore the curves of my breasts with their fingers. It feels so wrong, but it arouses me. Then one of the blond-haired girls climbs up on the chair, mounting me, and kisses my lips. Then she runs her tongue along my tongue, French kissing me. She puts her arms around me and whispers into my ear. The sound of her whispers, and the others' kisses along my body, echo in the chamber, as if mixing with the sound of the rhythmic drums. I've never even kissed a girl. The short-haired lady runs her lips along my cheeks and neck, grinding her body against mine. Behind her, I hear something far more lewd. The two naked men I saw before aren't just kissing, like the girls, they're groping each other and moaning. Are they having sex?

"Drink," the short-haired lady whispers in my ear. She licks and gently bites my ear. "Drink and you will be free from inhibitions. Drink and all fear will fade. Do whatever you wish."

"Whatever you want," says the man, nodding. His back is still turned to me. It's as if he's staring at the lake through the windows before him. "I initiate you under the light of Lucifer, our morning star."

The three girls are all over me, fingers gliding over my naked skin.

"Go away, girls," I say quietly. "I don't want this."

They don't. And half of me doesn't want them to stop either.

Then I'm surprised to see a man's bald head under me. The woman who was sitting on my lap disappeared. The Head Priest has dropped down on a knee, and he runs his lips over my stomach and kisses my inner thigh. Then he runs his tongue over my pussy, while the other women continue to kiss every part of my skin. I feel fingers enter my pussy. The man? And all the while, in the background, I still hear moaning from the other two men.

All three girls step back and offer the chalice again. Together they hold it up to me.

"Drink."

I take the gilded cup and sip. It's a salty and metallic elixir. It tastes gross. I spit up. But then I'm presented with the gilded chalice again. I drink more, as their hands tip the cup into my mouth, forcing more down my throat.

"Look down upon the altar as your sacrifice flows, initiate," says the man under me. "Amen."

I feel something warm run down my legs.

Looking down, I see blood trickling down the altar.

And then I hear the sound of a baby crying.

~

"Oh my god, Bryce!"

"What's wrong?" Bryce says sleepily. "What's the matter, Cadence?"

"God! God!" My eyes open in darkness. No...not darkness. I see the ceiling of my bedroom and our window, overlooking the forest under the night sky.

"It was a dream...but it was so real. But it was just a dream. It was horrible."

I gaze at our backyard through the floor-to-ceiling bedroom windows. Then I quickly turn away. Our backyard is where we perform ceremonies. The last thing I want to see is a bunch of people in black cloaks.

"I dreamt I was at that secret house in Scotland partaking in some sex ceremony, Bryce. But that's not all. The leader killed our baby."

"What are you talking about?"

"It felt like a curse to kill our unborn child, Bryce. I don't know. It was so real and that's what I felt. I was dreaming that I was having a miscarriage, and I think it was from occult magic. It was after I was offered this disgusting elixir. Maybe the elixir was given to me to kill her? It was some elixir to initiate me to Baphomet, but it also killed Chandra. It felt so evil."

"It was just a dream, Cadence."

I sit up and put my head in my hands. I start crying.

"Cadence, you were studying demonology all night," he says, rubbing my back. "It was probably just all that studying."

"I feel violated," I say, shaking my head. "It was like when Melanie attacked me in my wandering, but this was Scotland. It felt so real, Bryce, too real. And...I don't know, I think our unborn baby was killed. I feel so afraid. It's like when I had the prophecy about our daughter but, this time, I feel like they killed her."

"Cadence," Bryce says. He holds me as I shake. I'm crying. I'm trying not to, but I am. "Will you stop saying that? You were studying Crowley. You were asking for something like this to happen. You've been reading the occult like crazy for days."

"For my research," I say with a nod. "I told you about that letter. I messed up so bad with Dr. Bainer, I feel like if I could just show the other professors, they'll take me back. If I can prove I'm worthy. Now, after seeing how sick Kenosha was in the hospital, and that letter, I'm sorry to tell you, but I don't think I'll be in Hawthorne next year."

"You might not be a graduate student, but you'll be here no matter what," he says gently. Then he massages my back. "We'll figure things out, whatever happens. Don't worry. We'll cope. No matter what, Cadence, we'll be fine, even if that happens. Don't worry about it now."

"I'm scared, Bryce." I turn and snuggle in his arms. "I'm so scared. Why did Alondra say she wanted Enora to show me her magic? All her magic is dark. I don't get it. It's like the dream. I don't ever want to learn her dark magic. Just like I don't ever want some black magic initiation."

"You might have dreamed that stuff, but I did it once, Cadence. Remember? I was part of those ceremonies."

"I know, babe. We talked about it. It's over for you."

"It was just a dream, Cadence."

I turn on my back and stare up at the dark ceiling again. I either turn to Bryce and cry more, turn to our chair and empty wall, or look straight ahead, through the window, at our backyard. All I can do is look up. To God? If God would only be there for me.

"We need the grace of God, not the devil, Bryce," I say. "Alondra's wrong this time. Frida has the right idea."

"Was it Alondra? Kenosha keeps thinking some dark spirit from the Samhain Witch possesses you and tricks you into thinking it's her. Melanie was celebrating turning you bad when she made you cast an evil spell. Maybe she wants you to go further this time?"

"It was Alondra."

"Or maybe it was Enora making you say it?"

"It was Alondra. And Alondra was agreeing with Enora. Enora, Bryce. Why the hell would she do that? Maybe her spirit thinks I need to learn backward magic to fight whatever's fighting us? I don't know. You saw what Aunt Jane said. Jane's right. If Alondra herself never taught me, why should I learn left-sided magic now?"

"Maybe you should call Liam?"

"Liam left because of all this stuff. I already know what he'll say."

"But if anybody knows what Alondra meant, it's him. Maybe he could teach you instead of Enora?"

"No," I say, shaking my head, "Liam cares about us, but he'd never teach me a thing. You know that. He doesn't want to come anywhere near Hawthorne anymore if he can avoid it. No, Bryce, we need Frida's grace of God now. God, not demons or devils."

"Amen."

"God, don't say that. Enora kept saying that with her weird lover slave, Aamon."

"What can I say to help you back to sleep then, babe?" he asks, actually chuckling.

"Nothing," I say, slapping my forehead with my palm. "Just nothing." Then I run my fingers through his short hair. "Forget it. Go back to sleep. I'm sorry I disturbed you."

I squeeze my eyes tightly to try to calm down. But now all I hear in our bedroom is Bryce breathing. But I like that. I like him lying beside me. From the corner of my eye, I see him just staring at the ceiling in darkness.

"Babe, are you sure it was a spell?" he asks finally, after a long silence. "Our unborn child? Jesus, Cadence, you're scaring me too. Is that another prophecy?"

"I don't know. No, it was a dream. But attacking people in nightmares was Enora's thing, remember? It seems like Enora's dream casting, not Melanie's power. But Enora hardly seemed strong enough to curse me after the attack." I shift to the side of the bed, away from him, and try to close my eyes. "Forget it. Goodnight, babe. I don't want you to be too tired for your lecture tomorrow."

But it doesn't take long for me to pull off the covers and jump out of bed. Who am I kidding? There's no hope for sleep tonight.

I dare myself to do exactly what I'm afraid of doing. I walk over to our large floor-to-ceiling window and look outside at our backyard. Why? It's like our sabbaths. I'm not going to let fear get in the way of the things I love. And I love this view of our backyard more than anything else in Hawthorne.

Our bonfire, surrounded by the shadows of trees, is lit violet. This happens every night, but I don't tell anyone anymore. Otherwise, it's dark outside.

I whimper. I can't help it. I don't want to cry, but I do. Then I feel Bryce put his arms around me from behind. I heave a sigh, lean back, and cradle my head against his chest.

"Hi," I say.

He doesn't say anything. He does something better. He lowers his head and touches his lips gently to mine.

"Sorry," he says. "Can't resist. You're still freaked about the dream?"

"Don't say sorry for doing things I like, Bryce," I say with a chuckle. "Yeah, I'm totally freaked out." I turn and reach up on my tippy-toes to French kiss my lover. "But this is what I need. Not the horror of that dream. You." Our lips touch again. "But you need rest."

"I'd rather be up with you."

"Well, I should warn you. My confusion might be casting a spell on you. After that dream, my magic could be like a wandering."

"No spell makes me desire you more than I already do."

"I love you so much, Bryce."

He runs his hand over my black silk nightgown, down my back, and over my butt. And I feel tingles. Then he squeezes my ass and I love that. I touch his ass. I move my hand up to his well-built abs and chest. He's so fit. So hot. I stroke his hard chest while our tongues keep dancing. He squeezes my lower back and my ass again. Then he takes off my nightgown. He pulls down my panties and caresses me.

"You're not too sleepy? But you have that lecture tomorrow."

He chuckles and shakes his head. "As long as Alondra's not inside you."

"We've been through this already," I say between kisses. "Allie was discreet."

"Allie, Cadence?" he asks, stepping back.

"Shh... Don't ruin the mood."

I yank down his underwear—easy enough—revealing his hard cock. Then I kiss his lips again and stroke his penis. And we stand here in darkness before our huge floor-to-ceiling-window, looking over our backyard and smooching, caressing each other, pleasuring each other. And it's wonderful.

Somehow, we end up in bed. I'm lying on my back, and Bryce is on his side kissing me like crazy again, caressing me, running his hand along the curves of my breasts, squeezing my nipples, doing exactly what I want him to do. Then he is on top of me. I can't see the window, or anything but my husband on top of me. And we just kiss as his hard cock slides along my leg. That makes me desire him more than ever.

He enters me and it's electrifying.

"Oh, Bryce."

He thrusts inside me so slowly and gently. I wrap my arms around him tightly as he moves over me, as if I'm keeping him from escaping. Then, again, he's touching his soft lips to mine. He runs a hand along my neck while I caress his hard, muscular back and arms and run my fingers down to the crack of his ass. His tight ass clenches as he thrusts into me.

"Yes, fuck me, Bryce," I say softly. "Fuck your wife."

And he does. But he's gentle.

We haven't been using condoms. At first, it was a surprise and unplanned, but now it's like an unspoken plan. Bryce and I would love a child, I suppose. But that makes me think of the nightmare again. What if that dream *was* real? What if I'm going to have a miscarriage now? *God, what if I have a miscarriage from a spell cast by Enora and her evil coven!?*

"What's the matter, Cadence?" Bryce asks. He stops. I didn't realize that I had stopped moving too. "Is it the dream again?"

I nod. Then I'm afraid I could stupidly start crying. That would be so dumb and mean.

"Just keep going," I say. "It's okay, Bryce. Don't stop. Why don't you just finish?"

He shakes his head. "Not if you don't want this."

"But you want it, right? Aren't I pretty enough?"

He laughs.

"There's enough light from the window to see me. And you're not finished."

"You're prettier than anyone I've known. Of course I want you."

"I'm just thinking. I'm doing too much of that lately. I'm thinking of—"

"The dream."

"It's just a dream. Like you said."

But he stops again.

"You're right." I thrust up a little. "It's okay. Everything will be fine. Just finish, babe."

"No, I won't if you're not making love to me."

No!

I throw him on his back. He's in shock and doesn't say a word. Bryce is probably two times my weight, so I suspect my being able to throw him down was influenced by a little magic. I'm not sure why I'm being so violent. But, for some reason, I want him more than ever now. It's almost as if it is because he was going to stop. Or to reward him for being such a wonderful man? A man I love more than anything in the world? I don't know. But now I want him more than ever.

"We need to fuck," I say.

I grab his cock and guide it inside me again. And now I'm the one riding on top of him. I'm moving fast and hard. I'm pounding up and down on him, and I hear the mattress creaking. He's hardly objecting. For a second, he actually laughs. Then his fingers are squeezing my soft skin, pressing me into him, squeezing my ass, wanting me more than ever.

"Yes, fuck me, Bryce!" I practically scream.

That makes him stop again. Why? I think he's shocked that I'm screaming.

I'm pouncing up and down on him now. There's no stopping me. Then, again, I scream some more. I've moaned a lot before, but never this loud. I know there's no one else in the house. So...why the fuck not? Why not do whatever the fuck I want?

"Fuck me! I need this so bad. I want to have your baby, Bryce. I want to fuck you so hard! I want to make a baby! Let's do it, tonight. Don't you want to? Don't you want me now? Come and fuck your wife. Let's make Chandra."

That thought drives me to push into him harder than ever.

"Shh, babe," he says. "What's gotten into—"

He can't say anything else because my mouth covers his lips. My tongue runs along his. Then I guide his fingers along my tits. I take one of his hands and start sucking his finger. He squeezes my breasts while my hips move up and down like crazy. Sweat drips from my back down the crack of my ass. I'm breathing so heavily. This is like a workout. I lean down again and press his lips so hard. Then I grasp his head, pressing my lips tightly over his, nearly hurting him as he tries to breathe. I'm pressing so hard into him, it's like I want to go through him or something. I want to be closer than ever before. *I love him so fucking much!*

He takes my head in his hands and tries to push me away, but I smack his hands from my face.

"No. Fuck me."

"What's going on with you, Cadence?" he asks with a laugh.

Yeah, why? Why am I acting like this? It's like I want pain. It's like an animal was let loose into my house and it's fighting to pleasure Bryce. He's smiling but he seems confused. So am I. But... It feels so good... Then it feels like he's not moving again. I don't know.

"Cadence, what's the matter?" he asks, out of breath.

"What do you mean? What's wrong? You want me to stop?"

It feels as if...as if I feel like the answer to that horrible nightmare is to conceive. Or to just fuck the shit out of my husband. The thought of conceiving a child with Bryce is almost more important than the pleasure itself. Even hurting him would be okay...if I could...and...maybe it's because he was going to stop? I want him to have pleasure. I want him to feel good. He deserves it. I just want my Bryce, my hubby, to be happy. Is that wrong? Is it wrong for us to feel good right now?

"Cadence?"

"What, Bryce?"

Does he actually want me to stop? Are you kidding me?

I lean forward, close to his face, and run my hands along my tits.

"We need to fuck," I say, shaking my head.

A flash of purple brightens the room, making me squint. There must be magic in the air. Bryce is in shadows so dark that I can't see him for a moment. But I still feel the pleasure below. No, I feel it stronger than ever.

"We need to fuck."

"Babe?" he asks.

Really, all I see is violet. I hear him, but all I see is the blinding purple light shining in our bedroom.

"What?" I ask, panting. "What is it, Bryce? I love you so much."

"I love you, Cadence."

"Then what's the matter?"

"Nothing."

My head hurts. I have to get this to end. I have to finish him off. I can't do this forever. It feels so good, but it's too much.

"Cadence, why don't you slow down? What are you doing?"

"No, take me! Fuck me! Do it now. Don't you love me?"

"Of course I love you. I love you more than anything."

"Do you want me to stop, Bryce?"

"No. But calm the hell down." He chuckles nervously again. "What the hell's going on?"

"Oh, Bryce! Take me. Make love to me! Fuck me!" I shout, like some ravenous animal. "Fuck me!"

I want to devour him. And it's all because I love him so much. I love him so fucking much! I want us to do whatever we desire. Whatever gives us pleasure. I want his happiness. I don't give a fuck about mine. It's all for him. It's for him to do whatever he desires to be happy. And what's wrong with that?

"Are you almost there?" I kiss him.

"Yes."

That's finally what I want to hear. It spurs me to bounce on him more than ever.

"Yes. Yes! Fuck me. Fuck me now, Bryce! Come on! Just do it! Oh, I'm cumming. Yes. Fuck me! You and me. I think I'm cumming now. I'm cumming. Are you? *Fuck! I love you so much! Yes. Do it! Fuck...*"

All this coaching is finally enough. I feel him spent under me.

I fall by his side.

I'm so exhausted. I feel like I just sprinted a mile. Sweat is dripping all over my naked body. I blink and beads of sweat fall down my forehead.

"What was that?" he asks, panting.

"What do you mean?"

"That was so rough," he says with a laugh. "What's gotten into you? It just didn't...seem like you."

"But you liked it?"

"Yes."

I laugh. He laughs uncomfortably.

"I don't know. But it felt so good...right?" I'm still out of breath. I take a deep breath and turn on my back, staring at the ceiling again. "I don't know. You know, I think that was better than ever before."

8

———————

FRIDA

I'm sitting in a cubicle on the third floor of the Jonathan Brewster Taylor library, on the internet, sifting through everything I can find about Aleister Crowley. I have a stack of six books on this topic on my desk. I have to study.

Or do I? I'm getting canned, remember? Perhaps there's no point.

Well, I'm working three times as hard, holding on to that last part of my university letter that said the word *appeal*. Wasting time? Maybe. But Kenosha heard about the letter too. She told me she'd do what she could to fix things with the committee for next year. But then, typical of Kenosha, she hinted that *I need* to do everything I can with my final exams and thesis. *Hint. Hint.* I tell you, this so-called graduation committee is beginning to feel like her witch council. It's shrouded in mystery and feels almost as occult as witchcraft.

Anyway... Aleister Crowley. Did you know that Aleister Crowley was a mountaineer and traveler? Yep, and not only was he an avid reader on the occult, like yours truly, but he loved going to other countries and climbing mountains. I don't like that. I'm afraid of heights.

I'm looking at a black-and-white picture of the Boleskine House. The grounds around the Boleskine House look quite beautiful, and being that it's beside Loch Ness, there's more mystery in that home than just pentagrams. There's good ole Nessy, the Loch Ness monster, of course. (I think I'll have to get a super silly picture of the Loch Ness monster for a slide for my lecture; maybe it will lighten the mood while discussing Satanism).

Aleister Crowley was a nutjob. Or...was he? Maybe he got a bad rap?

On March 24, 1923, he was famously called the "wickedest man in the world" by a London newspaper titled *John Bull*. The newspaper reports that he impregnated two women in Sicily after involving them in ancient Dionysian rituals. The said rituals were performed in triangles and circles, and they were influenced not only by ancient Greek rites, but by Kabbalistic and Egyptian occult magic. He was accused of sexually violating women drugged with hashish before sacrificing live goats. The article goes on to accuse Crowley of recruiting professors from Oxford and Cambridge for his cult practices (that sounds familiar). And, I further surmised, from other sources I studied last night, that the greatest source of trouble occurred in 1923, when a man in his cult died of liver failure after being forced to drink tainted water. This gentleman had been forced to ritually cut himself every time he said the word "I." These were just Crowley's famous exploits in Cefalu, Sicily. It was all enough to have the dictator Mussolini expel him from Italy.

What about before? When he was a boy, myth has it that he tortured and killed the family cat in order to *scientifically* determine whether it had nine lives. Another tale tells that during one of his million perverted affairs, he published a set of poems titled *Adultery*. I'm sure his paramour appreciated the public revelation of their affair. Word is, his own mother thought he was a demon-child.

And yet, many of these tales, interestingly, were told by his enemies. Perhaps his reputation was poisoned by the media because he took pride in thumbing his nose at society. That was the whole point of his new religion in Thelema: freedom. See, unlike Anton LaVey, he wasn't really a Satanist—he was an anti-religionist. He proclaimed himself the "beast" and evoked the number 666 to rebel against Christianity. Many of his rituals, including his famous Gnostic Sabbath, proclaimed that each member in ceremony was a god. Although this was vehemently antithetical to Christianity and the love for God and Jesus, it holds a great deal in common with the modern new age movement. Yet during a more religious time, in the early twentieth century, his statements against Christianity were highly inflammatory.

And yet, here's the thing: he wanted to sue *John Bull* for libel. I find that fascinating.

I turn to the window by my cubicle. All I see is our millions of trees and a clear blue sky. The weather's been lovely, but still a little hot. I suppose I could have met my friend outside?

Then I turn to more papers on the subject. Many of these papers in the library were sent over to the university by, you guessed it, Alondra. Yep, my old teacher was fascinated by Aleister Crowley too. There are many passages about him in *Broomstick*.

According to other reports, Crowley was a drug addict—addicted to a lot of bad stuff like cocaine and heroin. And hashish. (I didn't even know what hashish was until I looked it up last night. Apparently it's a stronger concentrate of marijuana.) Whether a beast or not, I think he was a pervert like Professor Reardon, addicted to sex, with his sex magick, with males, females, and animals. He was also thought to suffer from bouts of paranoia due to syphilis and gonorrhea—the same fate Al Capone suffered around this time.

But Aleister considered himself a prophet, who believed that using sex and drugs to exhaust and torture his cult members would lead to enlightenment. He believed getting the practitioner close to passing out would help them approach an enlightened state in Crowley's new religion, Thelema.

I'm thinking perhaps his religious drive was not so bad. I mean his *religious*, not sexual, drive. Like any religious leader, he was trying to understand our world. Like Alondra. Like me. Right? That's why I study the occult. Was he as evil as all these people say he was?

There are still practitioners of Thelema in the world. The best explanation I can come up with for their beliefs is that they're trying to shake off religious guilt and feel free. He didn't worship Satan; he worshipped a shapeless demon named Choronzon. He wasn't about worshipping Satan; he was about religious freedom. Whether you consider Aleister a villainous beast or not, this distinction has to be understood to fully get him. I intend for my students to get that point in my lecture. Judging from Alondra's comments in *Broomstick*, she understood this. But for many believers in Christianity, there's really no difference anyway, I suppose.

"Hi, Katie," says a girl with a Brazilian accent. It's Frida and she sounds terrible.

"Hey, Frida," I say, jumping up. I hug her. She barely wants to touch me. "I miss you, so much. Thanks for coming."

She nods.

"What the hell's the matter?" I ask.

Frida wipes tears from her eyes with the back of her hand. Then she grabs a chair from another cubicle, lays down her bag of books, and sits beside me.

"I'm sorry, Katie. I've really been wanting to talk to you."

"I know. I've been trying to reach you. What is it? What's

going on? You haven't been answering your phone again. Then you didn't show up at Beltane."

"I..." She turns from me and faces the white wall of the corridor. Her hands are shaking. I reach over and rub her back. I think that makes it worse. I hear a whimper.

"I'm leaving, Katie," she says quietly.

"I know. You're graduating."

"No. I mean, I'm leaving witchcraft. I think I decided back when that old woman passed. I just didn't have the heart to tell you. But now, after what happened with Enora... I'm not only leaving our coven, I'm leaving witchcraft. I don't want to have anything to do with being a witch anymore."

"Okay, if that's what you want. You're not the only one who's not happy being a witch. I love our friendship. That's what's important, Frida."

"It's not what I want. I love you, Bryce, and Maddie, but things are getting worse in Hawthorne. You know I was initiated after Maddie. I never saw the horrible stuff that happened to her. If I had, I would never have joined. Then the explosion and fire almost killed us when Alondra made you High Priestess."

"Sorry 'bout that," I say with a chuckle.

"No. No one got hurt. But then, later, you were turned into a snake. I told you how terrible that was. I remember looking for you every day with our friends under the deck of your home. You don't know what that was like, Cadence. And then we had the huge fight with Enora on campus. And then Mira was almost killed. And now... And now..."

"It's okay, Frida. I know it. Forget it."

"It's just all too much," Frida says, shaking her head. "It's too much. What happened to that poor old woman, Agnes, should never have happened. She was so sweet. If witches are good, why would something like that happen to such a sweet old lady? I don't understand it."

"I know. It was terrible."

"No. You don't understand. I... I saw you cast the spell."

And *that*...that feels horrible.

She quickly puts a hand up, but it's too late. My cheeks feel warm. I am really pissed. Frida's so sweet, she never hurts anyone—intentionally—but coming from her, saying out loud the guilt I've felt all along, is, I think, one of the worst things anyone's ever done to me.

"I know it was out of your control, Katie," she says, "but seeing you do it upset me so much, and then hearing your voice change, and then seeing Alondra cast that spell and hurt that frail woman." She pauses to wipe her eyes again. "I never liked Alondra. If she's inside you, I'm sorry, but, Cadence, I was afraid of her." She pauses and just puts her head in her hands.

She shakes her head and loses it. I reach for her, but she moves away.

"I got into witchcraft because of my curiosity about magic. I love magic. I love magic, because I love the spirit of magic in religion. But I believe in evil, Cadence. You know my brother, Liam, is a priest. My family is religious. I believe in the devil. Perhaps that makes everything that's been happening worse because I believe our group is a part of the devil's work now. I feel like, gosh, I feel like you're changing too. You keep saying you're worried about becoming evil, but I feel like you want to be evil. Why aren't you doing anything to stop it if you're so afraid of it?"

She still has her head in her hands. I think it's because this is the first time she's ever really confronted me about anything.

"Maddie told me that ghost in you asked you to learn magic from Enora," she says. "Why would you do that?"

"I know, Frida."

She still has her head in her hands and just shakes it.

"I go to church," I quip.

There's something about saying those words that makes me regret it the minute they come out of my mouth. I think it's because there was bite to my tone. Because, you see, if this were Maddie, or any other friend, I'd be screaming right now.

"If you really believe you're doing evil things, you have to stop them."

"I know, Frida."

"No. No, you aren't going to stop," she says, looking up with bloodshot, teary eyes. "You keep saying you will, but you won't. Maddie told me that Alondra told you to practice black magic. Like...*sex...magic, Katie?*"

She can barely say it. But she does. And that does it. I close my eyes and squeeze my hands so tightly. I'm seething.

"Why would I ever do that?" I snap.

But Frida just lowers her head in her hands again and nods, morose as hell.

"Frida! Frida. Alondra is inside me because Hawthorne is in trouble."

"I don't care, Cadence. I'm sorry, I can't do this. I still love you, but I can't. I just can't do this anymore." She jumps up.

"Okay, Frida. Fine. But there's still a month left in school. No more sabbaths with the group. You don't have to go. I'll let the others know. I'll just see you in church."

"No, Katie," she says, shaking her head, her words breaking. "No, I'm sorry, Cadence. I really wish you well, but, but no, I can't be anywhere near you anymore."

What!?

"Bye, Katie."

"You hypocrite!" I shout.

She whirls around.

"Frida, you go to church, but then you joined Alondra's satanic cult. You might not have been there when all that stuff happened to Maddie, but you heard about it. You knew what you were doing when you joined. You shouldn't be afraid of me, Frida, you should be afraid of yourself. You're already going to your hell, whether you talk to me about it or not."

Frida stares at me in shock. Tears are still flowing from her bloodshot eyes. I don't think I've ever even raised my voice at her before.

"Bye, Katie," she says quietly.

She rushes off down the hall.

Fuck! this hurts. This hurts so damn much!

9

———

WHISPERS

I'S DARK. QUIET. I'VE COVERED ALL THE WINDOWS OF MY GUEST room, locked all the doors, and switched off all the lights. It's a clear day outside, but I don't want to see the sun. It's as dark as night. I have one candle burning, and I'm speaking to you in a whisper because I don't want to disturb my peace. My peace feels fragile, as if any sound, touch, or even smell could make me afraid again. Fear. That's what this is, this fear—I feel so afraid of...fear. Even though I sit here cross-legged with my Book of Shadows, *Broomstick*, by my feet, I feel very afraid.

What am I scared of? Why am I afraid? I'm afraid I won't be numb. I'm afraid that I'll lose this newfound bliss. I'm afraid to feel. And if I do that, and then I discover what I'm really afraid of...

10

DINNER OR WHATEVER

I'M SITTING IN A LARGE BOOTH STARING AT A SMALL FLICKERING candle on my table, which is covered with a chic white table-cloth. Only about half the booths in the restaurant are full, because it's still early. It's dark, aside from the candle, and its flickering light feels romantic.

I'm wearing a formal black dress, and I curled my long hair. I applied "pretty" makeup, not gothic, with red lipstick and brown mascara. I look good. I should. I spent like two hours getting ready back home. But I feel nervous. Over the last week things have been getting weird between Bryce and me. The last time we had sex, it was a little weird, as you might remember. And then he and all the sisters in the circle heard about Frida.

I've been sleeping in the guest room lately. I'm not mad at Bryce. Or... I don't think I am? At first, it was a way to get him to sleep in bed. He kept falling asleep in the dining room with the excuse that he didn't want to wake me. Now, after a couple weeks, I think it's becoming something totally different.

Speaking of Bryce, there he is. He's near a podium by the front door asking a sharply dressed hostess where I'm sitting. She points at my table and I wave. He looks so cute. He's wearing his lovely dark suit, a white shirt, and slacks. I picked out those clothes for him. The hostess is wearing a white suit with suspenders and her hair in a bun. She grabs a menu and Bryce follows her over.

"Here you are, sir," she says with a smile. "Enjoy."

Bryce leans over and kisses my cheek. "Hi, hun. Happy anniversary."

"Hey, babe. Same to you. I hope this booth is okay? Booths are what you like, right?"

"Whatever you want, Cadence. Sure, it's great."

And he sits across from me and smiles.

"I was worried you wouldn't make it."

"Huh?" he asks, furrowing his brow. "Why? What are you talking about? We never had our anniversary dinner." He touches my hand. "Happy anniversary, babe. I'm so happy to be married to you."

Then he runs his fingers through his perfectly combed hair. He smiles and stares down at the one-page laminated menu. He doesn't need to. We've been to Lacey's a thousand times.

"I think I did well on my anthropology exam. It was multiple choice."

"Oh, that's great, babe."

"With that over with, I can focus more on Dr. Stoferson's class. His is all about the final. And, of course, yours. You know, I can still bring up my grades so they're good enough."

"Kenosha will grade our class, Cadence," he says with a nod, staring at the menu.

"Yeah. Um-hmm."

I look around.

There's the most well-behaved kid I've ever seen in my life. The girl's wearing this cute blue bow and a maroon and sky-blue dress. She looks like she's only three. Dad's quietly cutting pieces of steak while her mom is spooning some soup.

"Psst," I say quietly. "Look over there, Bryce. That kid is so cute."

Bryce glances up from his menu, but he doesn't have time to comment.

"What would you two like to drink?" asks a young lady. She's also wearing a white suit and suspenders.

"I'll have a Coke," Bryce says. "What about you, Cadence? You want anything?"

"No."

Shit, I'm trying to get pregnant. Doesn't he remember?

"I'll have...a Diet Coke, I suppose."

The waitress nods. "Okay. Well, you two let me know when you're ready to order. I'll be back in a few minutes with your drinks."

"Not sure she likes that," I say almost in a whisper, cupping my hand beside my mouth, as she walks away. I laugh, hoping some levity will lighten up the mood. It doesn't. He furrows his brow, looking more annoyed than ever.

"We don't have to drink to have steak," he says with a shrug, still looking at his menu.

"I know. I didn't say I was offended, I don't care, just she looked like she was. Hey, do you see that cute little girl over there, Bryce? Look. Over there."

Bryce glances over and nods.

"Hey, why aren't *you* having a drink?" I ask. "You always love red wine. This is our celebration, Bryce. Why don't you go all out and have some?"

"It's okay. But I was thinking the same for you, Cadence."

"Bryce..." Does he really not know? "We're *trying*, remember?"

"I know we're trying," he says with a shrug. "But let's not talk about our problems tonight. Let's make this night special, Cadence."

"Huh?" I open my eyes wide and shake my head. What the hell is he talking about?

"No," I say, shaking my head. I gesticulate with my hands out. "I mean, *trying*, you know, *trying* for a family? No alcohol for me, you know. *Trying for a BABY?*"

"Oh." He nods and chuckles. "Oh, yeah." But he doesn't seem to like that much either.

This dinner is already not going well. I don't know, I feel uncomfortable. I thought finally going out with Bryce would make things better between us. He's cute as hell in the suit he's wearing, I guess. That's something.

"But why aren't you drinking?" I ask again.

"Cadence," he says, shaking his head. "I don't know how to tell you this." What? Jeez, that sounds so horrible I'm not sure I want to know. "We don't have a lot of money."

"We don't have enough money for our anniversary celebration?"

"No, Cadence. We don't. You know, Uncle Hanley might be letting us live in an amazing house, but we don't have a lot of money. I just repaired my BMW. That car was used when I bought it five years ago. It's ten years old now. Your Jaguar—again, thanks to Uncle Hanley—is great, but it's old too. Fortunately, the school's helping pay for your graduate program, but both of us have debt from college. And with your recent letter about the program, who knows next year if—"

"Okay..." I bite my lip. "Fine." My cheeks are feeling warm because I think I'm getting mad. "But this is our celebration dinner, Bryce. An important celebration for our first-year anniversary. We just got married a year ago. You said you wanted to do more than just have breakfast."

"I didn't bring it up. You did. You asked why I ordered a Coke."

"God, I wasn't aware our money was so tight. I can get a job, Bryce."

"How? You're barely passing graduate school."

I quickly turn from him. He's not wrong, but that really stings.

I recognize an older man in a gray suit, short and bald. He is Dr. Garson, my economics professor from a few years ago. He's sitting with his wife. I doubt he remembers me. But I don't want to look at Bryce because, *though true*, what he said felt real mean.

In the far corner, I see an open window. It's still bright outside. We planned our dinner for before sunset, because we don't like crowds and Lacey's is truly the only steak house in town. But sitting at one of those tables might have been less confining than this booth—especially if we're about to have a heated fight. He's the one who likes booths. I actually prefer tables and chairs.

And now he's back to staring at the menu he's memorized. I almost feel like I'm sitting across from Dr. *Brainer*.

"Frida's really hurt," he says, suddenly sounding pissed. "You need to talk to her. If you want, I can talk, but you're our High Priestess. You can't ignore what's happening."

"Bryce, I really don't know what the hell is happening with her. I did reach out. First I met with her for dessert. She acted like everything was fine, but then she still didn't show up at our sabbath and church. Or at Beltane. Then this week, she met with me to study and went whacko in the library."

"She told Helen you yelled at her." He finally meets my gaze, looking seriously pissed. "*Frida*, Cadence? *Frida?* I've never seen anyone yell at Frida. If you're under a curse, then you and I and our friends need to help you."

"Who said I was under a curse? Frida said she wanted nothing to do with me anymore. I never did anything to her. I just shouted at her after she told me that it was all my fault. I thought that she was being pretty mean. Then she ran."

"What are you doing every night in the guest room? I'm

hearing spell casting." He runs his fingers through his hair again. "I've heard you screaming. I spoke with Maddie. We even came by your room one night and listened at the door. You were yelling incantations, acting like you'd completely lost your mind."

"So now you two are fucking spying on me?" I ask in a forced whisper.

"It's our house, Cadence," he says, shaking his head. "You're the one shutting down, screaming, and acting weird."

I squeeze my hand tightly. The candle snuffs out. That only seems to make Bryce more pissed.

"You're so distant lately."

"Every night," I say, seething, "I come home and you're busy studying in the dining room. Every night. Every night. Some nights, I'm not even sure you sleep. When I come by, you wave or nod your head. I'm not the one who's abandoned his wife."

"*Abandoned his wife?* When the hell did I do that? Why would you say such a thing, Cadence? I think you're under a spell. You're not acting like yourself. Or is this Alondra talking?"

"No, ai'ght!" I cry, hitting the table with my palm. "I'm not Alondra." A few people look over. "It's me! And I'm not under a spell. I'm just getting really pissed with you right now."

"Will you quiet down," he says in a hushed voice. "Jeez. You've been muttering things downstairs behind a closed door, Katie. Maybe it's all this occult research you're doing. You're studying practitioners of left-handed magic. Are you casting their spells?"

I put a palm up. I don't want this to continue. I just know this is only going to end badly.

Then I look at my hand. It's my left palm. My fingers move into the shape of an "okay" sign. I've heard plenty of rumors about the meaning of that shape. Some say that's the figure of a six, as in 666.

Hmm...maybe I am losing it? I'm admittedly getting a little

weird—or weirder than usual. I've been moonlighting doing quite a lot of occult research, but that's because I'm desperate not to fail out of school.

The waitress comes over with too big a smile. She seems to be in the greatest of moods, kind of the complete opposite of us. She hands us his Coke and my Diet Coke in ornate crystal glasses. I sip some. There's a nice amount of fake sugar in my drink.

"Do you two know what you want to order yet?" asks the waitress.

"Well, I do," I say with a smirk. "I've seen your menu a hundred times. He has too, but he's still staring at it."

Bryce squints, looking like he wants to reach over the table and slap me. "Still looking," he says, giving me a nasty smirk.

The waitress leaves. Then I become a full-on bitch with a large grin and toast to him.

"To us. Happy anniversary, Bryce."

"You hurt Frida, Katie," he says, shaking his head. "You hurt her bad."

"How did I hurt Frida? Bryce, I told you she came over to me crying her eyes out. I did nothing to her. She just told me she doesn't want to be around me anymore. How is that my fault? So, yeah, then I yelled at her back. But I barely yelled. Was that so wrong? She made me mad. Just like you're making me mad now. I've been under so much stress since I was your student, as a sophomore, in this weird fucking town."

"Fine. Just keep it down, Cadence."

"Now you're acting like a dad again, Bryce. You've heard a mouthful over that already. You're so authoritarian lately."

"No," he says quietly, "we're in a fancy restaurant and you're shouting obscenities."

"Well," I say, practically in a whisper, "now I'm failing out, right, fucker? So I'm doing my best to keep things together, Dr. Wallace. With Enora, our class, the coven..."

He blinks hard and takes a deep breath. "Why don't you order a real drink and forget it, Cadence? Fine. We're both under so much stress. You're right. As always. Just get a glass of wine or something."

"You sure we actually can afford one?" I ask with a shrug. "Or is it that you want to kill our unborn child?"

"*What!* Why would you say that, Cadence?" he asks in a whisper. "Look, I forgot. Okay? God, if you're not under a curse, I don't want to be anywhere near you right now. You've been acting so crazy. We have to stay together as a family. Why would you hurt the most nice, innocent girl I've ever known? You're acting so cruel to Frida."

"I didn't do anything to Frida!" I cry. "She's messed up in the head because now she's locked into thinking that any witch is evil and against her religion, Bryce. And that includes you, warlock!"

"I don't know what's going on with you," he says, shaking his head. "Now with that letter and you leaving next year..."

"I thought you told me we could work things out?"

"I did. I do, babe. Of course... But—"

"But what?" I stand up.

I don't know what the hell has gotten into him. *I'm under a spell? What about him!*

"Sit down."

"No," I say, picking up my purse. "No, this isn't what I want." I wipe my wet eyes with the back of my hand. "I'm done."

He gets up too and puts a hand out to stop me.

"Please, Cadence. Forget it. I'm sorry. Forget everything I said. Just sit back down."

"No. I'm leaving. I'm going to save you some money."

I rush to the parking lot. I hear the door open behind me. I'm totally sure my husband is trying to bring me back into the fancy restaurant he can't afford. But I don't let him catch up to me. Instead, I jump in my Jaguar and peel out of the parking lot.

As I drive onto the road, in the rearview window, I see a flash of light strike the forest. It's a sudden brilliant light under a cloudless sky. It's as if some army is attacking us with a missile strike. But it's not a missile. It's Windstorm in her full magical, witchy glory. The explosion erupts into flames among the trees. I watch the smoke rise behind me through my rearview window as I drive back home.

After another half mile, the smoke is still growing.

I hope it fucking burns down that fucking restaurant! Come to think of it, next time I'll have the lightning bolt directly hit the roof. Lacey's? I mean, *Lacey's?* Maddie was right, I should have fucking left Bryce after he took me there more than once in the first place. Especially after he proposed to me there. I'm under a curse? Me? I'm acting cruel? Well, if he's not under a curse, he just acted like a total fucking asshole.

11

NUMB

I'M RUNNING.

And boy, as I huff and puff like a maniac, I can tell I'm totally out of shape. I used to work out every day, but not lately, with all the recent witchy weirdness. You know, after a while, you get used to that extra day of free time without sweating.

It's dark as hell outside. I'm running during the witching hour, and white wisps of clouds rush overhead past a full moon. The moon looks like an auburn halo. I love that. It's a little misty. It's also oddly warm. I think it's like eighty degrees, and that's making me sweat in the darkness. It was way too hot during the day to go running, you know. That's why I'm running in the middle of the night.

Right?

I rush under a thick forest canopy, and I worry about twisting my ankles in the dark. I can barely see under the thick foliage. Then, after I pass a tranquil waterfall, I climb another trail into an open field, and the full moon lights my way, making this wild grass lovely.

I have to run. I just have to. Okay?

But I feel terrible. Why is this happening? I mean, it has

always sucked in Hawthorne, right? Or has it? As much as I've complained, bawled my eyes out, or felt completely nuts, I think things are only getting worse. Losing friends like Frida makes me feel worse than I've ever felt before. I mean, I lost Maddie last year, but Frida! *Sweet Frida?* Bryce is right. Who the hell fights with Frida? I knew she was leaving for New York by the end of the year, but I wanted to part by hugging her and loving her sweet smile and her happy-go-lucky self. Not fighting her and being accused of sex magic.

Fuck!

I'm pissed.

But...you know...I already miss her. You never really know how much you'll miss someone until you lose them.

My phone buzzes in my pocket. It keeps buzzing like crazy. Fuck off.

I climb another hill. I am so tired, but I almost feel like I should be enduring this pain, like somehow I deserve it. I don't know, I just feel like I deserve punishment for all the terrible things I've done in my life. But what have I done?

Frida said I was evil?

It's just like you, Alondra, and your relationship with Liam and Jane. You lost them when they became afraid of you. It's funny because I've always felt like Frida looked up to me but, really, I looked up to her. I've never believed in God. See, I *wanted* to believe in God. I wanted to have her faith. That's why I keep going to church. But now, I suppose there's no reason to go to church anymore.

I approach a stream. The water's higher than last time. There's only one way to cross it, and I'm not about to turn around. So I carefully step in the water with my white tennis shoes. My feet feel so cold under the slow current. Then, as I trudge farther, the wetness rises right below my bare knees. I slush through. Just before I almost dip down and start swimming, I pass the middle of the stream. But a shoe gets stuck in the mud as I run to the shore.

Kenosha looked so sick in the hospital. Why did I tell Dr. *Brainer* off? Can you be any stupider, Cadence? Maybe you could do with a "brain" right now, stupid? What the fuck were you thinking? That was so dumb.

I'm running up a steep, grassy hill, between shadowy bushes and trees. Yeah, it's creepy. I suppose I should be a little scared running in the middle of the night. Some huge bear or mountain lion could attack me. But I remember the summit of this hill is so gorgeous with a bright full moon, and I haven't been up there this late before. That white moon is so large, it's like Diana beckoning me, forcing me to climb up despite the pain in my legs and hips and the cramp at my side.

My phone buzzes again.

Fuck off!

This trail levels off, and I meander past more trees.

It's quiet here. I hear just the sound of my drenched shoes clapping over more puddles and slushing through muddy leaves. I don't feel magic, like I would in a witch wandering. But I also don't feel afraid. I feel numb.

I finally reach my destination. It's the peak of a hilltop with a stunning view of the woods below. This is even higher than Hilltop Bluff, the tallest peak within hiking distance of campus. I look down at miles upon miles of Hawthorne Forest, the trees looking like shadows under the starry night. Though the sky is still splashed with white clouds, the full moon is now free of clouds among Astraeus, the god of the stars. And the stars are so vivid and pretty over my rural town. In one corner, far below, lies Hawthorne Lake, and mountain ranges loom in the far distance. But right below my muddy tennis shoes are just treetops, as far as the eye can see. It looks like if I jumped five hundred feet, my fall would be cushioned by all those leaves and tree trunks.

I want to jump. I'm not suicidal, okay? I just always feel like jumping when I'm on a really high spot like this. Don't know why. Maybe you think I'm weird because of that? (You probably think I'm weird due to a lot of other things).

Last year, I forced my BFF to accompany me here. That was in the afternoon, under sunlight. I was sad because Maddie was telling me she was leaving me this year. Well, at least that never happened—ironically, due to our fighting. She stayed in Hawthorne over her love for my brother.

Well, tonight it's just me in this clearing, staring out into the shadows of the woods below in the middle of the night. So what do I do?

I shout as loud as I can. It's so random, but it feels wonderful! So raw. So refreshing. I just shout and scream as loudly as I possibly can. It reminds me of the last time I had sex with Bryce. It feels primal. Free. Wonderful! Like I can just do whatever the fuck I want.

The phone buzzes in my pocket again. I finally give up and answer it.

"Yeah," I say, out of breath. "What?"

"*Where the hell are you!*" shouts Bryce. "You're disappearing again, Cadence! I've been searching all over our backyard. I called the gang, but no one knows where you went. Are you in a wandering? Is this all about Lacey's?"

No, it's not fucking about Lacey's. But I answer by shouting as loudly as I can at him. Maybe it's Bryce's fault for reminding me of our fight at the restaurant? I don't know. I'm still mad at him, you know. But that's not why I'm screaming into my cellphone. Why? Because I can. I can do whatever the fuck I want to do out here in the woods, and no one will ever know. Only my hubby, my love, can hear me.

I wish he were here to enjoy this beauty with me though... Is he still on the phone?

"Bryce? Bryce, are you there?"

I think I hear crying. Bryce? That's weird. I don't think I've ever seen this man cry before.

"Bryce? Are you okay?"

"No," he says softly. "No, I'm not okay, Cadence."

I look down at those trees again. The bushes and leaves are shadows. Then I wonder, can I fly? I'm a witch, you know. I've levitated before. But can I fly? Can I take a broomstick and skim over those leaves and branches?

"Cadence, I told you never to leave me again."

I laugh. Then I say, between guffaws, "But Frida left us, Bryce. Not me. Frida's gone. Sweet and kind Frida. But it's okay. It's okay because she doesn't want to be my friend. Not just our sabbaths, she doesn't want to be anywhere near me, Bryce. Sweet Frida left us. And I'm never going to be the same again. You know why? Frida's afraid of me, Bryce. She's afraid of all of us!"

He doesn't say a word.

I listen to the chirping crickets and a nearby animal rustling through leaves in a bush. It's so quiet.

"Please come home," Bryce says quietly. Then he hangs up.

I shout and rage again atop my mountain. Why? Because I can. I can holler, I can scream, I can do whatever I want to do in this life! And no one can stop me!

My phone buzzes in my pocket again.

"Cadence?" It's Maddie. She sounds so tired, like she just woke up.

"Huh?"

"Cadence, Bryce just called. He said he's looking for you. Is everything all right? We're so worried about you."

I laugh. Then I scream. I yell as loudly as I possibly can at the phone. Then I hurl the fucking thing over the precipice.

It flips and drops straight down into the shadows. It takes a while to fall. I watch moonlight reflect on the glass. I watch it take forever to fall below the trees.

But then...oddly, it doesn't disappear. I squint and see it hovering among the tree branches. It glides as if being pushed through the air like a feather. Then it slowly climbs until it is level with me, about twenty feet away. I reach out. The phone gently glides right back into my palm.

I chuckle nervously.

"Cadence, are you there?" asks Maddie. "Cadence?"

I shout at Madison some more.

12

——

HER MAGICK SPELL

I roll out of bed. It's five o'clock. Five o'clock in the evening. I slept all afternoon. I make my way downstairs and head to my living room. Bryce has been out all day in meetings and lectures. He never came to me last night in the bedroom. I think he's beyond angry at me at this point.

I sit for a while on the sofa staring at a wall. I yawn. I'm so tired. I muster just enough energy to open my laptop, on the table beside me. I've already set up an appointment for video conferencing with Enora. That's the only reason I bothered getting out of bed.

It'll only cost me twenty dollars to video conference with her in jail. Apparently, she hasn't turned into a bird and flown the coop yet. Maybe she knows a way to get me out of my misery?

I'm under a witch's curse now. Okay? Sure. I get it. Don't you think I know that? I was with you on the cliff yelling like a banshee. I'm either suffering from a complete mental breakdown or I'm under a wicked witch's spell. Or perhaps both?

Am I mad at Bryce? Sure I am. But I get why he's mad at me.

And school? Am I angry with Hawthorne U.? You bet I am. Frida? Every time I remember her crying in the library...over what? *Me?* Every time I picture her crying, I get more and more mad at her. I really don't regret yelling at her anymore. Honestly, I think I should have shouted at her more.

So...yeah, I'm probably under a curse. But I have every fucking right to be. Last year, I helped my friends Mira and Maddie get out of their curses. Who's gonna help heal me?

Enora.

You probably think that's a crazy idea but, after seeing her condition in the hospital, I just know her accident wasn't her doing. Everyone has tried to get rid of Melanie—you know, cleanse "mud"—and no one I know besides Enora can help me finally stop that witch. Even Liam needed my help.

Am I crazy? Maybe. But I'm desperate. Is it a curse or is it losing my marbles? You tell me.

"Oh, hi Katie," Enora says with a wave and her usual irritating ungenuine smile. She looks awful. Enora's a pretty girl, prettier than me, and I've always hated her pretty face, but now she's not wearing any makeup. She's got bags under those lovely eyes, and she's in an orange jumpsuit.

"You look tired," Enora says, ironically. "What can I do for my least favorite witch?"

"I was surprised to see that you hadn't flown away yet."

"Shh," Enora says, putting a finger over her lips. "Well, I can't talk about *me*. I've got other reasons for putting up with this joint. They've got all these lies about my coven that I have to stop. But don't worry, I can talk to you about dark magic. That's why you're calling, right? No cops believe in hexes, jinxes, or curses so it's safe to talk about that." Then she looks over her shoulder. "But, actually, you want to know something absolutely fascinating, Katie?" She leans forward with a huge grin. "One of the guards is actually a witch. Shh. You know what I did to him?"

I shrug.

"I fucked him. Yeah, I fucked him real good." She falls back in her chair, holding back laughter. "He was real good. We snuck into the supply room down the hall. You want me to tell you his name?"

No. Why the hell would I care?

"Carl. Officer Carl." Then, for some reason, she guffaws like crazy. She looks right into my eyes and says, "Got that, you motherfuckers? It was C-a-r-l on my cell block. Ask C-a-r-l what he was doing in the supply room with one of his prisoners. He's hot as hell, tall, buff, and loads of fun, but somehow I don't think guards are supposed to screw their inmates. Ask him why he left his post. Check the cameras. We walked into the kitchen supply room down the hallway, and I showed him some personal *sex magic*, Katie, if you know what I mean."

"Enora, what the hell are you talking about?"

"I'm not talking to you, dummy," she replies dismissively. "They record these videos... So..." She backs up and just gives me her sly grin. "What evil can I teach my least favorite witch?" She laughs. "Alondra asked me to teach you, eh? You want me to show you my magic? Honestly, it surprises me. I never thought you'd listen even to her about learning secrets of Baphomet."

"I don't want to learn anything from you, but..." I turn from her and throw my hair back. Then I take a deep breath. I lean back on my couch and fold my arms. Then I think that, as bad as things have gotten, at least I'm not in jail. *Yet.* "I think your magic is the only way to fight my curse. I haven't been acting myself. I'm ignoring everyone, screaming from the top of my lungs, and wanting to jump off cliffs. I've been rude, even cruel, to people I love. I've kind of...acted like you, actually. I'm pretty sure Melanie's not only fighting you, she's cursing me."

"Surprise, surprise. Of course Melanie's cursing you. What do you expect? We're the most powerful witches in town.

Melanie is hunting each and every one of us. That's how I met Aamon. He was feeling her wrath too. Well, it's time to fight back, Windstorm. I told you, I can help. But there's gonna be a price."

"I know. You want Melanie dead."

"Cadence," Enora says, shaking her head. "Cadence, shut the fuck up, won't you? Who kills people? Murder? Honestly, how vulgar." The bitch laughs again. "Who would ever do such a thing? What did I just say about this video meeting and the law?" But her grin becomes wider. She puts her hand to her chest. "You know, I would never want to hurt anybody. I'm talking about *magical* witchcraft."

"How do I do one of your spells?" I ask, rolling my eyes. "Just sip blood or kill a squirrel?"

"Easier. I have to initiate you with a blindfolding spell. We'll arrange a circle. You may use chalk, just get your ass inside the pentacle. Take henbane or mandrake, preferably, but even whiskey will do. Then put on a blindfold. After six hours remove the blindfold. Then you'll be free." She turns for a second. She looks back with her stupid condescending grin. "Voilà. Magic."

"Are you fucking kidding me? I just wear a blindfold for six hours?"

"No, I'm not fucking kidding. You're a witch. You already know magic. You just need to try Baphometic magic. I tell you, Cadence, my spells are so much more satisfying."

"How is covering my eyes going to do anything?"

"Do you have any idea what a blindfold will do to your head? Sounds simple? It's dangerous. In hoodoo, it's done with an oungan, but I've officiated over the casting before. Things get very strange without sight. The most important rule is you can't remove the blindfold before the allotted time or the spell fails. That's the hardest part. You can't remove your blindfold."

"So drugs and a blindfold. Fine. That's all? And then I'm powerful enough with dark magic to take care of Melanie?"

"No drugs. Drugs are illegal, Cadence. Come on, you know better. *Legal* herbs or alcohol." She grins stupidly again. "Yes, the magic will empower you to finally help me. It's all about me, Cadence. Maybe my spell will teach you something. I really don't care. Whatever happens, you will help me by paying me back. You will meet with another witch and cast magical jinxes on muddy-bitch. Our magic together will stop the Samhain Witch. I need one witch to hold her, the other to take care of her with black magic. Your initiation is best done with a sexy red satin blindfold and a legal concoction to get you fucked up. But the blindfold is it. Of course, it's not really it. There are incantations, but I'll help you with that.

"I'll send you an email about where Raven will meet with you in person next week. Some like to fuck initiates during the initiation to enhance the conjuring—hence the sexy blindfold —but I have a feeling you're not bad enough for that." The bitch cackles again. "But let me know by email. I can probably arrange a healthy young stud for you if you'd like. Alondra did that many times. She didn't initiate me, of course, that sick fuck Bill Reardon did. And he did lots of improper intercourse during the ceremony, I can tell you. It hardly helped me. Anyway, trust me, you walk around without being able to see anything for a while, and you'll start seeing things. Add your power over spells, and things are gonna get pretty...*magical.* Just make sure whatever you do, you leave the blindfold on for six hours. The most difficult thing with this spell is resisting the urge to open your eyes. If you hold out, the gift will be worth your time. This is all based on an ancient voodoo initiation practice in dark magic. Just make sure you last six hours. Don't skimp on six. Keep your eyes blindfolded for six hours to block your senses. Doing it for six hours three times would be even better, if you prefer, because then it'd be like, you know, six, six, six—" She laughs and raises her left hand, showing me her pentagram tattoo. "Hail, Satan."

"Okay."

"Okay. Your meeting with Raven will take place under the waning half moon at the center field, the very center, of Meadow Park. *Raven* will meet you just before midnight. Just remember the cost. We're gonna take good care of that bitch. I'm still in a lot of pain. Honestly, it's comfy enough here, but the fuckhole doctors don't like giving me pain medicine. And, Jesus, look in the mirror. Get some sleep, won't you? You've got a curse, all right."

"*Raven* as in Mira?"

Enora's smile is larger than ever. "*Raven*, as in you-know-who, stupid."

"Will it rid me of my evil curse?"

"Cadence, you can't damn the damned."

"But it'll help get rid of the Samhain Witch's power over Hawthorne?"

"Yes. Yes. It will do those things."

"Fine. Bye."

"Oh, don't eat or drink anything for six hours before the meeting either."

"Fine. Goodbye."

"And fast throughout the week. No meat. No sex. All week. You should be abstaining and doing that all the time for your sabbath, but I know the type of witch you are. See you soon, Windstorm. Don't forget that, when the time comes, you'll owe me."

"Bye."

"So nice of you to visit me in prison. Give kisses and regards to Willow. I'll pay her back soon enough as well."

Then the bitch raises her right palm to wave goodbye. That

sends a shiver down my back. She's raising the hand with stretched, deformed skin—the one I burned last year. And as she raises her palm, her smile looks more sinister than ever. I get the innuendo.

The screen turns blank.

13

———

ROAD TRIP

I'VE BEEN DRIVING NONSTOP FOR SIX HOURS. THE WEATHER'S TOO nice to stop. It's not too hot or cold this spring. It's really lovely weather. I mean, I'd rather be walking, but the luxury seats in Alondra's gray Jaguar are super fab. I've got one companion on my impromptu road trip, aside from you. My book: *Broomstick*. Don't think I'm crazy enough to go out on a ghost haunt without it.

Where am I heading? White Hill, Missouri. That sweet couple that showed up on my doorstep was looking for protection from the Hawthorne Witch, remember? I remember. I even spoke to that ghost hunter, Raymond, on the phone after I promised Mary I'd come and visit. Ray told me how much he used to love working with Alondra back in the '90s. He said he once witnessed Alondra speaking to a transparent specter in a cemetery. I told him I was familiar with ghosts myself.

I wonder if Bryce remembers this ghost haunt? He warned me to stay home—at least not to go to the haunted house until Kenosha was well enough. I don't know, who cares. I feel really, really good this afternoon. But I'm in big trouble with my husband when I get home. Especially being that I just showered, quickly changed, and took off on this journey without saying goodbye to him.

The phone rings as if hearing my thoughts. It keeps doing that. I dig into my pants pocket and take it out. Yep, it's Bryce. And there's like a hundred texts from other people in my witch circle.

I stuff the phone back into my pocket.

The freeway is deserted. Everything along the highway is so flat here. The land, covered in wild grass, with a few trees, seems to go on forever. It seems like I drive for miles and miles on one- or two-lane highways, just staring at dead trees and weeds. But I actually like the flatness. It's something I never see back home in my woods.

When I was a teenager, Mom and Dad took Damie and me on a trip through Kansas to Colorado. I'll never forget all those flat landscapes, all the way to the horizon. It was so pretty. Seeing the view without anything blocking it is kind of like the freedom I felt screaming on top of that hillside overlooking Hawthorne.

I'm tapping my steering wheel to Stone Temple Pilots. It's a slower song, "Black Again," and that reminds me of Mom. She's probably the only one who could have gotten me out of the funk I'm in right now. Mom loved grunge music and got me into Smashing Pumpkins and System of a Down. I love that heavy shit. I learned from Liam that he and Alondra used to love the Smashing Pumpkins. I'm always finding stuff that Alondra and I have in common. It's funny because I used to think Alondra and I were like oil and vinegar.

I pass the state border sign.

So now I'm in Missouri. That means I should almost be there. White Hill is a town at the southernmost tip of Missouri, close to Tennessee.

I pass a large green sign reading "White Hill." It says the population is 2,272.

Then I'm off the highway, driving on a one-lane road into this super-small town circle around a large brick building. There are just a few shops and restaurants here in their "down-town." And I thought Hawthorne was small. I look at my navigation and take another right onto a very desolate looking dirt road. My navigation says I'm almost there, but all I see are more flat fields with bushes and sporadic trees.

Then I see a sign with the address I'm looking for beside a wood fence. In the far distance, close to the red glow of the setting sun on the horizon, I can just make out a small white farmhouse.

At the end of the road, I park my car behind a large white van near the house. It has a screened front door and quaint cottage windows. And a huge dog is barking like crazy behind the fence in the front yard. A Great Dane, I think. (I don't really know dogs; you know, I just know cats.) There's no grass, but in the distance I see a small field of green rows and a tractor.

The phone rings and buzzes again.

I grab my book and quickly get out of my Jaguar.

And then...I stretch. The phone's still ringing and buzzing incessantly. I sigh and reach into my pocket. For the first time, it's Dad.

"Hi, Daddy."

I tilt my sunglasses down and squint, taking a better look at the one-story farmhouse silhouetted by the setting sun.

"Cadence, where are you?"

"I'm fine, Dad." How am I going to explain all this to him? "I had to just take a drive and get away. Things are getting a little strained with my friends back home, that's all."

"Maddie and Bryce told me you were screaming like a madwoman on the phone in the middle of the night last night. All of us are so worried you're in a wandering. Are you? Wher-ever you are, I can come pick you up. Are you near the college?"

No, I'm a bit farther from campus.

The sun is setting. It's so pretty. The flat ground with the red sun in the distance—it's something I just can't experience in the woods back home. I put my shades back down. Then I clutch my grimoire closer to my chest and squeeze my fists tightly. A *wandering*, Dad?

"Why do you know what a wandering is?"

"What?"

"Why do you even know what a wandering is, Dad?"

"Katie, are you near campus? Or your house?"

"How can you come get me? What are you still doing in Hawthorne, Dad? You live in Atlanta. Why do you keep asking Aunt Jane about witchcraft? Better yet, Dad, why is it that you're still in town?"

A heavyset older man, with a mustache and suspenders, gets out of the large white van in front of me. It has dark-tinted windows and all sorts of antennae on the roof. Of course, all my questions for Dad are rhetorical. But asking them is only getting me angrier. I know damn well why Dad is living in Hawthorne.

"Cadence, is this the time to talk about this?"

"Yes, Dad, I think it's the perfect time. I'm just far enough away to not accidentally hurt you with the magic you're not supposed to know about. That's why Frida left. She's scared of me, Dad. Maybe you should be too?"

"Cadence..."

"You want to know what my friends and I are up to? I'm an evil witch. You saw Alondra's green eyes. That was nothing. You have no idea the shit I'm going through. The shit you're now getting yourself into by staying in that fuckhole town called Hawthorne. Why don't you go back home to Atlanta? Why are you even—"

"Cadence. Please..."

"No. No. Do you know what happened to Maddie last year? I couldn't accept Damien going out with my best friend, but it wasn't only our fight, she was in the middle of a witch's curse. A real witch curse, Dad. And now you're hanging out with Maddie's mom? Even though Aunt Jane's been married like three hundred times? And even though she's more of a witch than I am? But you won't talk about that. You'd rather have secrets. Well, Dad, secrets are evil. Occult. And I hate secrets more than anything in the world."

"Cadence, I know... I..."

"You want to know the truth? A week ago, I had a dream that I was having sex in a sex cult. I dreamt that an evil cult leader made me bleed and have a miscarriage while women were having sex with me." I'm fighting tears now, but I'm not going to cry. I just won't do that. But my voice is breaking. I'm so pissed! "It was Bryce's and my unborn child, 'kay, Dad, that black magic killed! Dark magic killed our unborn baby. So? What else would you like to know, Daddy? Then Frida, the nicest angel in the world, really the nicest person I've ever known, told me she's too scared to ever see me again. So I went out for a run at night. So? I'm a grown woman and I can do whatever the fuck I want. I ran up some hills, looked out into the darkness toward Hawthorne, and thought of flying over the trees with my broomstick. But I didn't. You know what did fly, Dad?"

"Cadence, just calm down. I just want to know—"

"*This fucking cellphone! This very goddamn phone, now enchanted, that I'm using right now to speak to you! This phone is back in my hand after I hurled it over a hill, and you can hear me, can't you? How? By real magic! Do you know why? Because I'm a witch. I'm a fucking cauldron-stirring, broomstick flying, motherfucking witch! And you know what? I'm evil! So scram!*"

I pause. There's just silence on the phone. The heavyset man is standing near me, but now he's keeping his distance.

"Is this Alondra or Cadence?"

"*This is your daughter, Dad!* I'm disgusted by what you've

done, okay? You know all the hell I was put through last year, but you chose to fall in love with a witch in Hawthorne anyway!"

"Jane is a good person."

"I know she's a good person. Fuck! I have to go. Sorry, but there are some good people claiming to be haunted by a ghost in White Hill, Missouri. That's where I am. White Hill, Missouri. There are no words between us. Regarding Aunt Jane, you've let me down. Okay? And you've let Mom down. Mom just died. All of Hawthorne has let me down. So feel free to stay at Alondra's house with Bryce. You can have our bedroom. I have to get away. Tell Maddie and Bryce, and the rest of our gang, that I just had to get away from all of you!"

And I hang up on him. In the past, it would've made me break out in tears. I'm sad but...no...no, not this time.

"I'm Raymond," the guy says hesitantly, approaching me and putting a hand out. I shake his hand as I put the phone back in my pocket.

"Hi, Cadence Wallace," I say. I take off my shades. "The Hawthorne Witch. Hi. So, tell me...is this the real thing, Ray?"

He stares at me real oddly. Then he shakes his head. "I'm not sure. I've been testing the EMF signals. It's possible. There's certainly enough limestone beneath the foundation. And..." He points to the wires over us and a pole beside an oak tree near the house. "There's large enough power lines. That's creating a lot of psychic energy, I think. Bo, the teenage boy, is the focal point. There's been word of some possible possessions with him. I'm thinking poltergeists, but I'm not sure. This one could be fake. You can check it all out and tell me."

"I have no idea what the hell you're talking about," I say with a laugh.

"Oh, sorry, you threw me off. Alondra used to ask me that same question. Your makeup and demeanor remind me of her."

"I've been told we're similar."

"Connor told me you were even living at her house? Allie and I had a lot of history together. She helped fund my work, including that van over there. We probably visited like a hundred haunts together. Even after our escapades, she still helped my business. I have one of the best practices in the world investigating the supernatural—thanks to you. Have you checked out my videos on YouTube?"

I shake my head.

"They're popular, if I do say so myself. I also had two documentaries made. And I'm still getting funding from Alondra's estate."

"I wouldn't know. Uncle Hanley's probably paying you. But Bryce is in charge of the finances."

"Who's Bryce?"

"My husband."

"Oh," he says with a nod. "So you don't know a lot about ghost hunting?"

"No, I don't know anything about ghost hunting."

"But you know magic?"

My phone buzzes again. I put a finger up, reach into my pocket, and grab it to turn it off. It's Bryce. Fuck him.

"Yeah, I know magic," I reply, stuffing my phone back in my pocket.

"Are you okay?"

"Huh? Yeah, fine. Why?"

"Nothing. You want to take a look at the footage? I've rigged cameras inside the house. I've been in White Hill for a couple days. I'm just glad you made it. It's really out in the middle of nowhere, isn't it?"

I follow him to his white van.

"Six hours from Hawthorne," I say. "Yeah, it's far. But it's nice to be away for a little while. Do you have anything to drink?"

"Yep. Inside the van. Come on inside."

14

———

CAT

RAYMOND OPENS THE TWO BACK DOORS TO HIS HUGE WHITE VAN. It reminds me of the cockpit of a spaceship. Everything is tinted with red lights, and he's got monitors all along the sides of the van and wires strewn across the floor. The monitors are showing everything from black-and-white to yellow-and-red images. There's a long, thin mattress leaning against one wall. I'm guessing this is where the guy sleeps? By the two front seats are a ton of bags, video cameras, wires, and microphones.

Raymond reaches over to a small refrigerator and hands me a water bottle. Then I notice we're not alone. A young woman with long blond hair is sitting in the passenger seat. She's staring down at the cellphone on her lap. It's dark in the front because a blanket is covering the windshield and front windows.

The girl turns. Her head is bald on one side, and a pigtail is on the other side. She's wearing lime green suspenders over a white shirt and black jeans. And she has bright green eyeliner and bright red lipstick. She's young, a teenager, I think.

"Cat, say hi to Cadence Wallace," says Ray. "The new Hawthorne Witch. She's our boss, so behave."

But the girl falls back into the passenger seat, staring at her phone, ignoring us.

"Cat!"

"What?" she asks, chewing gum. "What? Huh?"

"She's the Hawthorne Witch, I said. A real witch, Cat."

Cat gets out of her seat and climbs to the back of the van, crouching down to avoid hitting her head on the ceiling. Then she sticks out her hand for me to shake.

"Real witch, huh?" she asks, squinting. Her breath smells like cherries, and she won't stop smacking her chewing gum. "Wow. Like an *actual* witch? Like Alondra?"

"Yeah," says Raymond. "She's a real witch."

"Can you show me some magic?" she asks with a wink.

"Not now," Ray says. "Did you check the cameras, Cat?"

"Boring." Cat turns from me and rolls her eyes. "It's boring, Dad. Nothing's going on in this dreary house. I told you this was a bad lead."

"Why don't you show Cadence what we've got?"

Cat heaves a sigh again. Then she points to a black-and-white screen. It's a child's room. There's a small bed with a nightstand next to it. It's dark. This camera must be using night vision.

"Julie's room," Cat comments, pointing. Then she points to an orange and red screen. "Julie's room." And then she points to another dark monitor and rolls her eyes again. "Julie's room."

"Two monitors are infrared and one with night vision," explains Raymond.

"And this one's Bo's room," Cat says with a nod. She points to four other monitors, still smacking her gum. Then she swallows and says, "Here's the kitchen. Here's the living room. We've got cameras all over the house, except the bathrooms." She turns and smirks. "I told Dad we should rig the bathrooms." She laughs and winks. "That's where all the dirty stuff always happens in a house, you know. Where no one wants to look."

"Bathrooms are private, Cat," her dad says.

"Well, I give up," Cat says. "We haven't seen anything here all week. And if you think this van is cramped, you should see our motel room. So you're from Hawthorne University? Neat. From what I hear, that town is so cool. I've researched it for college. I would kill to be accepted to their history program next year. And Dad keeps telling me about all the real witches that go there."

"You're going to Truman or Mizzou," Raymond says. "That's final. Hawthorne is too far away from Mom."

"Not so far," Cat says. "Like Mom cares." She points at me. "Cadence just came from there. It's not that far."

"You're not going to Hawthorne University. That's final, Cat."

She rolls her eyes yet again. Then she blows a large bubble and pops it.

"I take my daughter on these ventures because she loves the paranormal," Raymond says to me. "She loves it more than me, I think."

"When it's *real*, it's real cool," says Cat. "When it's fake, it's an absolute bore, Dad."

"So what evidence do you guys have from the house?" I ask with a laugh.

"Zippo," Cat says.

"You have to be very patient with these haunts, Cadence," Raymond says. "It's not like tornado hunting."

"Oh, tornado hunting is fun," says Cat. "I used to do that with Steven and Chip around Iowa, Dad. You ever do that, Cadence? Tornadoes are loads of fun. A bit scary. You ever do it? I once saw an RV launch into a cloud in front of me. I'm not kidding. It was thrown from the road and flew right over our pickup truck. And trees got uprooted in front of our windshield. It was the coolest thing I think I've ever seen."

I shake my head. Cat shrugs and turns, blowing another big bubble.

"The boy claims to have seen a very tall dark shadow come out of his closet," Ray says, tapping on a black-and-white monitor. The screen shows a small bed, bookcase, and dresser. "This happened repeatedly until he finally opened his closet. He found a hidden door with walls painted with red streaks. There was even red smoke."

"Yeah," Cat interjects. "And green slime found by his mom in the kitchen. And more total bullshit. I mean, sorry, it's shit. Bull poop, I'm telling you."

"The boy's peculiar," Ray says. "He altered his voice when I spoke with him, and he sounded like a girl. Here's the best footage we've gotten so far."

"The boy's nutso," Cat adds. "That's at least fun."

Ray types something under the monitors. Another screen pops up showing the boy's room again. He pauses it. He points to a white glow on the screen by the closet.

"That's all we've got so far, Cadence," Ray says.

"Big zippo," says Cat, blowing another bubble. "That shade over there is known by those ignorant of the supernatural as dust."

"You're really not helping, Cat," says Ray. "Remember what I told you about who's funding all our stuff."

"It's okay," I say with a laugh.

"Just being honest," Cat says. "Sometimes we've seen amazing stuff, just not here, Cadence."

"We don't have many leads," Ray says with a nod. "But the boy is so spooky. When Cat and I investigated a couple months ago, Mary asked if there was anything else that could be done. I suggested the only other thing I could think of offhand. Alondra. You could tell how desperate Connor and Mary are when they showed up at your front door."

I nod. In another monitor I recognize Mary and Connor in

the family room. Mary's in a sweater and pants and sitting on the couch with their girl. The girl looks about seven years old, with long dark hair. Connor, the dad, in a T-shirt and jeans, has a hand in his pocket. He is drinking from a cocktail glass and staring out a window. I don't see Bo. No...there he is. I see Bo on another monitor, grabbing a cereal box in the kitchen.

"There they are?" I ask, pointing.

Raymond nods.

"Let me go talk to them," I say.

"But when do I get to see magic, Cadence?" asks Cat, snatching my elbow and winking.

"Stare into a mirror."

"Huh?" she asks. Then she turns to Ray. "What does she mean by that?"

Ray shrugs. But even that little tip makes Cat's lips curl into an excited smile.

15

MY DISTASTE FOR THE OCCULT

I accompany Raymond and his daughter to the front door. That huge black dog rushes by us behind the fence. Cat laughs, dips down, and reaches her hand through the fence to pet the dog's head. She's obviously crazy, risking being bitten. She also has to be real careful balancing the large camera, wires, and heavy bag she's carrying on her shoulder.

Mary and Connor greet us, opening the screen door. Mary has long blond hair and is wearing a dark blue silk blouse with jeans. Her husband has blond hair too, but it's cut short. He's dressed casually, in a T-shirt and brown slacks.

"May I introduce the Hawthorne Witch," says Ray beside me.

"Hi, Cadence," Mary says with a smile. "Thanks so much for coming."

"You have a lovely home, Mary." I walk inside.

From the entryway I see two halls on either side of a brightly lit corridor. Straight ahead, I think I recognize the family room I was peering at in the footage. Yes, that's it. We make our way down the hallway and enter the family room. Little Julie is on a brown sofa, already acting weird. She's in a cute red and green dress, but she's just staring ahead of her. I sit down beside her, but then I jump. Her whole body trembles.

"Julie, she's here to help us, darling," Mary says.

Julie vehemently shakes her head.

I take my cloak off and walk over to a gray lounge chair across from her. I thought that would help, but it doesn't stop the poor little girl from shaking. It might be because of my thick black makeup. I lay the cloak over my grimoire, on my lap. And then we all stare at Cat, who's standing over us with her huge camcorder.

"Do you have to do that?" I ask.

"I don't want to miss anything," Cat says behind her lens.

"You have cameras all over the house."

"Yeah, but the *real* story is you, Cadence." Then Cat blows another bubble and chuckles. "Witches and witchcraft. That's cooler than ghosts."

"Stop it, Cat," Raymond says. "Don't record her if she doesn't want to be recorded."

Cat turns her video camera away from me and points it at the girl. But that's far worse, because the poor little girl shakes even more.

"Not her either, Cat!" I snap.

"Oh, come on," Cat says, "I have to record this interview."

"Just keep it away from the girl and me."

"Would you like a snack, Cadence?" Mary asks. "Connor, can you get the tray of cookies I made?"

I nod and smile. Hey, I'm not objecting to cookies. I'm starving, you know, after that long drive.

Then Mary sits beside her daughter. That seems to calm her a little.

"You said you don't know much about ghosts?" Mary asks me.

"I don't know all the technical stuff that Raymond does. But I've seen ghosts. Many times. And I know magic."

Mary nods slowly.

"I'm scared, Mommy," says the girl, shaking and leaning on her mom's shoulder.

"She's come here to help us, darling," Mary says.

The little girl shakes her head. "She looks scary."

"I heard that there was slime in the kitchen?" I ask Mary. "And that your son saw ghosts in his room? When did this all start happening?"

"About six months ago," Mary replies. "I've walked in a couple times in the middle of the night, and Bo was shaking in his bed. There's a section of his closet that opens into a small secret compartment. It's full of red painted lines and symbols. Bo says the closet opens itself at night. We even installed a lock on it, but it broke open one night. When the ghost comes, the window in his room shakes. So do the walls. Bo won't sleep up there anymore. And...he's starting to wet his bed again. Julie, here, is starting to sleep in my bed at night."

"Do you know anything about the previous owners?" Ray asks, leaning on a wall by the kitchen door.

"That's what worries us. Apparently the owner was an undertaker working in the town's funeral home. We bought the house five years ago, after he died. The realtor told us that before we bought the house, but we didn't think much of it. Now we're worried that he's the ghost haunting my son."

Connor comes in with a tray of wafer cookies. I take one. Cat takes three before she's back behind her camera.

"Where's your son?" I ask Connor.

"Bo, you come out here now, hear!" hollers Connor. "We have visitors about the ghost. Where is that boy off to now?"

Bo comes in, staring down at a small computer in his hands. He's a pale boy, maybe twelve, wearing a black T-shirt and shorts. "Hi," he says, not looking up. When he finally glances up, he quickly averts his eyes from me.

"This is someone who can help, Bo," Mary says.

"Nobody can help, Mom. The house is haunted, and I don't want to go up there again."

"He sleeps in our room now." Connor comes over and puts an arm around Bo. "Sit down, son."

He traipses over and sits beside his mom and sister on the sofa.

"In our research," Raymond says, "we've found that teenagers can be the source of paranormal ghost haunts. Not that Bo is to blame, but it is interesting that the haunting is coming from his room. It could be that he's channeling the energy. He could be channeling a poltergeist, if he's empathic."

"But not the paint," says Connor, shaking his head. "Why are there red marks all over the closet? We don't recall seeing that when we moved in. And the closet is where all the activity is."

"We checked the closet, Cadence," says Cat, still holding the camera. "EMS is zippo. Absolute nothing. There's no energy coming from his room."

I'm staring at the boy, but he won't meet my gaze. Both kids are terrified of me, leaning in their mom's embrace. That makes me mad. It reminds me of Frida. Why would anyone be afraid of me?

"Your son could be the vector," Ray continues. "He could be empathic." Ray turns to me. "Do you sense power in him?"

"No."

That oddly seems to make the boy shake more than ever. As he scratches his nose, his hand is practically flapping. Then he looks down at his handheld computer game again. I can't help staring at him, scrutinizing him. I feel like he's as much a part of this mystery as the house is.

"Mary, can you take little Julie out of the room for a sec?" I say. "I'd like to talk to her brother alone."

This boy is up to no good. I don't know how I know, I just do. Ray asked if I sense power in him—no, I sense something else. Lies. He's not only afraid of me as a witch. He's hiding something. And I loathe lies more than anything else in the world.

Mary takes the little tyke's hand and walks with her out of the room.

I get up and put my cloak back on.

"Bo," I say, standing over him, "why don't you go with me to your room and show me your closet. The closet where you're saying the ghost keeps appearing?"

"Don't want to," he says, staring down at his screen. "There's nothing there now."

"Why not just show me?"

He shrugs.

"Come on, Bo, you hear?" asks his dad. "Cadence traveled very far to help us."

"Don't want to, Dad," he says, staring at his computer pad.

"You come upstairs now and show her your closet!"

We head upstairs. Bo can't stare at his screen anymore, because his dad swiped it from his hands, but he's not looking back at me. He's walking far ahead. Cat's carrying her heavy equipment behind me while Ray is holding this really weird pointy device in front of him that's making beeping noises like a Geiger counter.

"What's that?" I ask Ray.

"An EMF detector."

"You don't know what that is?" Bo asks, cocking his head back at the top of the stairs.

"No."

We reach Bo's bedroom, but he doesn't want to enter.

"Bo," says Connor, "come on now, show Cadence your closet."

"No," he says, shaking his head, "don't want to. She can see it herself." He wipes his nose with the back of his hand. "I really don't want to go in there."

"I'd rather you show me," I insist. "The sun just set. I don't think it's late enough for ghosts now."

"I won't."

Fearless Cat doesn't mind ghosts. She reminds me of my daring brother, Damien. She's already inside checking every corner with her camcorder. Connor switches on the light and, for a moment, it really excites Cat. Then she looks disappointed when she looks up from her eyepiece at the yellow light emanating from a ceiling lamp.

I walk to a window. Peering through a crack in the drapes, I see the family's large farm and dirt driveway. There's only a slight glow now over a dark horizon.

"Here's the closet, Cadence," Ray says.

Cat throws down some of her wires and bags. Now she's carrying only her large camcorder, and she leans on her knee inside the closet. She slides open a small compartment with her free hand. Cat's video camera lights the small open chamber. I get down on my knees with her and see all the red paint streaks the family spoke of. There are red painted stars. There's also a black book with a red backward pentagram inside. It's like Enora's grimoire, but unlike her frayed and worn black book, this one looks brand new. Someone's into occult magic in this house, either these owners or the owner before. Could it have been the undertaker?

"Magic, Cadence?" Cat asks, turning to me, excited. "Whatcha think?" Then she sticks that infernal camera in my face. I squint and practically smack it away from her. "A witch book, *hmm?*"

"Move that camera away or I'll show you real magic."

"Maybe I shouldn't move it then?"

I can't help but laugh, but she turns it away.

"This stuff wasn't here when you moved in?" I ask Connor, cocking my head back.

"No," Connor says.

"What makes you think your son didn't paint it?"

"I didn't," Bo says. "I didn't even know about this part of my closet." The boy doesn't elaborate. He runs out of the room and back down the stairs.

I bend down again, reaching into the small chamber, and pull out the book with the backward pentagram. Then I thumb through the pages. There are lots of sigils of demons from the Lesser Key of Solomon that I recognize. Hell, I've been studying so much mysticism and magic that I could practically draw those images. Later pages have some poetry in Italian. I'm guessing this is from the *Aradia*, or *The Gospel of Witches*. At the end of the book are a bunch of stray pages with messy handwriting. Some of it reads like a teenager's diary, talking about friends and dating girls. Way back when, I was given a fake book like this for my initiation. Later, I was given my real centuries-old grimoire, *Broomstick*. Well, I might not know ghosts, but I know witchcraft, and this book looks like something someone would buy at a novelty shop. It also looks like a teenage boy's introduction into the occult.

And then...*eureka!* I spot the date on the first page. It's dated this year. The family said they moved here a few years back. Bingo! *Or zippo*, as Cat was saying.

But this gets me mad. I drove nonstop for six hours only to find that this entire haunt is a hoax. I don't get it. Raymond seems professional enough. Why didn't he realize this is a sham? But then I recall that the family, not Raymond, approached me.

"I've seen enough, Ray," I say, getting up.

"What do you mean?" Raymond asks. "I haven't shown you Julie's room. That's where she's been hearing noises too. This isn't the only room with activity, according to the family."

"I don't need to see her room."

"Bo!" cries his dad. "You come back here now, you hear! Where'd that boy go?"

"I won't, Dad," Bo shouts. I think he's back downstairs.

"Your boy is lying," I say, turning to Connor. "There are no ghosts in this house. The boy set everything up to deceive you. The only odd thing Ray's discovered was Bo's closet, and he simply painted it when you weren't at home. This book is his occult diary."

"Are you sure?" Connor asks, taking the book from me.

I'm too pissed to answer. If I'm right, this boy is messing with everybody's heads, including mine.

I head back downstairs. The boy is sitting on the couch in the family room, again playing a stupid computer game.

"You lied," I say. "Why? Why would you do that to your family, Bo?"

"What?" the kid asks, shaking his head vehemently. "I didn't."

"How do you know, Cadence?" asks Raymond, entering the room behind me.

"He made up the ghosts himself."

"I didn't!" Bo says. He starts crying. "I can't sleep! My room is haunted. Dad, I can't sleep in my room! I see shadows at night and noises. She's so weird. Just tell her to leave. Tell her to go away."

"Why not show me these ghosts then?"

"They don't come when you're watching. That's what ghosts do. How can you help us? You don't even know the stuff they're using. The shadows come out at night, I tell you."

"Liar."

"Nothing's been picked up in our surveillance," Ray says with a pensive nod. "Nothing's strange except that closet."

"Shame on you," I chide Bo. "You terrified your sister and parents. What do you think this has done to them? Do you think magic isn't real? Do you think there aren't ghosts? Ghosts are no joke. They're very real."

"I know they're real! They're up in my room!"

"There are no ghosts here," I say, shaking my head. "Admit that you lied to your parents."

"What?" Bo looks at his dad. "Dad, just ask her to leave. She's so weird."

Then the boy starts crying. I squeeze my hand tightly. The lights in the room flicker. Connor looks around, stupidly thinking it's proof that there are ghosts here. That only makes me angrier.

"Tell the truth," I snap.

"Okay, maybe Bo's right," Connor says, walking over to me. He grabs me by the shoulder. "That's enough. Why not just leave him alone now."

"What the hell are you talking about?" I yell, yanking my arm back from him. "I tell you, your boy made everything up. There are no ghosts in this house. All you have is a very sick son."

Bo's bawling like crazy now. And his father, now holding him in his arms, is coddling him like he's a fucking baby.

"*Shut up!*" I shout. "Stop lying and making a scene!"

"Just go," Connor says quietly, covering his eyes and shaking his head. "Just leave our house. Thank you for coming."

"No. Not until he admits his crime."

"What?" Connor asks, looking up.

Connor looks like he thinks I'm mad. Well, I sure am. I drove five hundred miles for a spoiled, messed-up teenager. Of course, Bo isn't saying anything anymore because he's stupidly falling apart on the couch. It's total bullshit. I turn from Connor and just stare at the boy. When he looks up for a moment into my eyes, it makes him cry even more. Connor gets up, scratches his head, and touches my arm again. "Look, Cadence, I appreciate you coming over, but I think that you should—"

I yank my arm back and extend my palm at the boy.

"*Resurgo! Resurgo! Resurgo!*"

My spell raises the kid up into the air. He starts kicking and screaming as I will his body to float above the sofa. Mary and Julie rush into the room, screaming.

"This is real magic!" I shout. *"Okay?"* I have to practically scream to be heard amid the pandemonium. *"Magic with a 'k.' The spirit world is not a joke! Magic is not a joke. Do you understand, kid? Admit your crime to your parents. Tell them that you made everything up and set up this ghost haunt. Tell them about the book you bought. Admit your lies or I won't let you down!"*

"What are you doing!" cries Connor. "My god, put him down!"

I shake my head. "Not until he tells the truth."

And now the boy is screaming—for real.

"Cadence, put him down!" cries Raymond.

"Wow!" cries Cat. "This is amazing."

"Tell the truth!" I cry.

"Get me down!" shouts the boy.

"No. Tell the truth and then I'll let you down!"

"Fine, I did it!"

"How'd you do it? Tell everything to your mom and dad."

"I made it up. I did it, Mom. Okay? I did it!"

"Where'd you get that book in the closet?"

"Chris gave it to me to cast magic."

"And the red paint?"

"I painted the closet when they all went fishing."

"You painted your closet!" shouts Mary.

"I'm sorry!" He nods his head frantically. "I'm sorry, Mom. Please. Let me go! Please. Let me down!"

"And the shadows at night? And the noises your sister heard?"

"I hit the walls near Julie's bed. It was me. I didn't mean to do it!"

"Tell everyone now. Reveal your lies and I'll let you down. Have you seen a ghost in this house or not?!"

"No! No!"

I drop my arm. His body lands hard on the couch.

He is still crying. So are his mom and sister, sitting beside him.

"Don't waste my time again, Ray," I snap, storming out of the room.

As I make my way to the front door, Cat points her large camcorder at my face. "Wait! Cadence, Cadence, tell us how you made the kid fly in the air. That was so sick! Tell us how you—"

My stare forces Cat to drop her camcorder. The camcorder rises, floats before her eyes for a few seconds, and is hurled violently against the wall, again and again, until it breaks into pieces.

"Your footage in the van is gone too."

I head out the door. I'm so pissed! I think I'm as pissed as I was in Hawthorne.

It's getting dark, really dark, here—out in the middle of nowhere. Like at home, the stars are bright. I like that and it calms me a little. A half moon shines above in the clear, starry sky.

"Cadence! Cadence!" It's Raymond again.

I turn wearily.

"I didn't expect that, but that worked just as well!" Raymond says with a big grin and a nervous chuckle. "How'd you know that boy was lying? That was amazing. I had my suspicions, but I didn't know. He's still weeping and apologizing like crazy. He's confessing everything to his mom and dad."

Cat's running out of the house, not far behind Raymond.

"The book in his closet wasn't there when they first moved in."

"It wasn't? How do you know?"

"It's brand new," I say, shaking my head. "The date on the book is this year. The boy bought it when he started painting his altar with red pentagrams. The house might not be haunted, but his parents have a whole new problem. Maybe some of the "ghost" activity is their weird kid getting into the occult? Not only is he a prankster, he doesn't know what the hell he's getting himself into."

"Join me anytime, Hawthorne Witch," he says with a broad grin. "I'll let you know of our next haunting. And, yeah, I won't waste your time. God, I never saw anything like what you just did with that kid. Not even Alondra ever did anything like that."

"I don't think people are going to want my kind of help, Ray."

"Are you kidding?" cries Cat, running up to me. "You just saved them, Cadence."

"They believe their boy," Raymond says with a nod. "Mary told me to tell you that she's eternally grateful. They're not crying in fear now, they're crying in happiness. They are so grateful to you for revealing the truth. I mean, they're angry as hell at their boy and the boy is totally freaked out, but Mary and Connor know they can finally get out of this horror."

"They're happy," Cat says with a big grin. "Thanks to you."

"Great," I reply, opening the door to my gray Jaguar.

"Hey," Cat says, before I close the door, "can you show me how you lifted that kid over the couch?"

"No."

And I shut the door.

As I make my hasty exit out of the farm in White Hill, Raymond and Cat are still standing by their white van, in my rearview mirror, watching me drive off.

I'm supposed to feel good, I suppose. I helped that family? But I feel horrible. I don't feel like myself, to tell you the truth. Maybe it's that curse again? Or maybe I'm just nervous about meeting Enora tomorrow?

16

BLACK CANDLES

I'm wearing a pitch-black dress with a lace collar. It reminds me of a vampire. The outfit is Alondra's. I found it in her walk-in closet, my walk-in closet, a few months ago. I don't know why I chose it; it just feels right. It's pitch black, I suppose. And right now, I'm running black lipstick over my lips. My eyes already look super witchy with dark mascara and eyeliner.

There's a note lying on the guest room bathroom counter. *"I'm really mad at you, Cadence. Whatever's going on, we can manage, but we have to work TOGETHER."*

You know, I'm not the kind of person who likes to hash things out when I'm angry. I stew and ignore the person. But I'm not really that mad at Bryce—but he's furious with me. I think it has something to do with leaving the state without telling him. Or maybe it was standing atop that hill screaming in his ear on the phone? But I'm not angry, I feel numb. And I absolutely love feeling numb now.

I take a brush to my long dark hair for a final time, staring at myself in the mirror. I look good. So gothic and witchy. But I'm nervous as hell. I don't know what to expect. I could run into problems I can't even imagine. I suppose that's why I'm afraid. I have no idea what to expect from Enora.

I head through our empty hallway and gaze at the dining room down the hall. There's no light on. Perhaps Bryce is upstairs asleep? Well, it's a good thing he doesn't see me. I look too good, like I'm all dressed up to go out and cheat on him. Not to mention, if he finds out where I'm going, we're going to break out into another all-out war.

I drive to Meadow Park, a small park on the outskirts of town. I saw kids playing soccer on the grass when I drove by last night. There are not a lot of kids or families in Hawthorne, you know. Hawthorne is primarily a college town. Most kids live in the neighboring town of Flintwood, so this small park is one of the main hangouts for kids.

But no kids are here tonight. Not now. It's nearly midnight.

The large green field glows under the streetlights. The bright light draws my eyes to the center of the field. That's weird. Even though it's artificial, it already feels like it's all part of a spell. But it's also attention-getting. I would have thought Enora would not have wanted our black magic conjuring to be made public—or to be seen, being that she's still supposed to be in jail.

I park and follow her instructions, walking to the middle of the field.

There I stand on the green grass under all these bright lights under a dark, cloudy night sky. It's a bit foggy so I can't make out any stars or moon, but I know this is the right time because a half moon was waning earlier this evening.

"*Yatu*, Windstorm," says Enora.

I squint at the surrounding trees, but I still don't see her. No...she's there amid the shadows in the trees, approaching me creepily as always. And, weirder, she's wearing the exact same pitch-black dress. Over her shoulder is a large red knapsack.

She drops the bag at my feet.

"*Yatu*," I say hesitantly.

"Nice dress," she says, winking at me with a chuckle. "Alondra got me that same dress when we were *friends*. What a coincidence."

"How'd you know I'd be wearing it?"

She crouches down and pulls out candles, a golden chalice, a dark book with a red backward pentagram—her grimoire?—and a few smaller bags and a bottle.

"Magic with a 'k,' Kate," she says, opening a small bag. "Magic with a 'k.'" Oddly, that's exactly what I said to that poor kid when I had him hovering over his sofa. "Did you make sure to leave your book at home, as instructed? And all your nice friends?"

"Yes."

"Peachy," she says. She opens the bottle and pours some of its contents on the ground.

"What's that?"

"You don't recognize this bottle, witch?" she asks with a laugh. "It's Jack Daniels." She takes out a large bag and starts pouring white powder, probably chalk, in a circle around me. "I had a feeling you'd prefer alcohol over the good stuff. I have henbane in my bag, though, if you prefer? But I figured whiskey would be sufficient."

"Will whiskey work?"

"With my magic, I could give you water." Then she stands and does something very weird. She puts both her hands on my shoulders, searching my eyes. "Ready, little lamb? This is going to be *soooo* much fun."

"I still don't know if I can trust you."

She comes right up to my face and holds me in an embrace. "Your introduction to the dark arts starts now, bitch," she whispers. "*Aiwass*," she whispers in both ears. Then she kisses a cheek and says, "*Aiwass.*" She nods and kisses the other cheek, repeating, "*Aiwass.*"

Slowly but methodically, Enora lights each black candle on the grass. Even the sound of the stroke of the match feels as if it is part of my ceremony. She's arranging the large candles in the shape of a five-pointed star within my chalk circle.

And the magic has begun. That word, *Aiwass*, echoes over and over in whispers all over the woods.

"Is it private here?" I ask.

"*Aiwass*," she says with a grin. Then she puts a finger over her lips and nods. She lifts the whiskey bottle and unscrews the cap. Then she guzzles some of it down with a big smile.

"Wait," I say, putting a hand up. All the whispers from the trees stop.

"*What!*" Enora snaps, rolling her eyes. "What is it, Cadence? Will you keep quiet? You need to stay quiet and not break my spell."

"I can't drink that."

"Why the fuck not?"

"I'm trying."

"Trying to fucking do what, Katie?"

"Bryce and I are trying to have a baby."

I mean, we haven't said we're planning to have one, but it's implied. I can't drink alcohol. And I certainly can't take drugs.

With an ungenuine smile, she flutters her eyelids and heaves a sigh. "Witches shouldn't get pregnant. It weakens our power."

"Well, we're trying, 'kay?"

"What I have to do to simply kill a witch," Enora quips, more to herself. "Fine. Fucking just sip the goddamn bottle, okay? You and I hopefully hold enough power."

"How many sips?"

"One, bitch," she says, raising a finger. "Just one. Will that do for you?"

"Now?"

She shakes her head.

She goes back to circling me and pouring whiskey around the circle of chalk. She still has a finger up, making sure I don't yap again. She guzzles more herself. A lot more than a sip. Then she reaches into another bag and pulls out a red silk band.

"A lot of magic is based on the trust of the initiate, Cadence." She stands up and shows me the blindfold. "The fact that you *can't* trust me at all will actually enhance the power of my spell. Your hands will also stay free, to represent free will, but you cannot remove the cloth until I say if you want the spell to work."

"And you promise to only give me a sip of whiskey?"

"For little Katie's child, of course. I would never want to hurt your unborn baby."

"No. No way, Enora. Why am I even trusting you!"

"Because, Cadence," she says, rolling her eyes again, "this park is a part of your hallowed ground. You could make a tree branch fall from a tree and impale me. If I dare give you more than a sip, just stop me and kill me on your grounds. All I'm going to do is make sure you don't impale *yourself* or sleepwalk off a cliff."

"Fine, Enora."

"Peachy."

Then she gestures for me to turn around. I turn and feel her put the blindfold over my eyes.

"Remember, no matter what's happening, don't remove this blindfold. That's really all there is to it. But you mustn't take it off, no matter how much you desire to."

"You're not going to do anything else?"

"Sit cross-legged and shut the fuck up now, 'kay Katie?"

I sit. Then I feel the bottle on my lips.

"Now, no biting or impaling Panthera," Enora says with a laugh.

I taste a sip of the alcohol on my lips. There. For the spell that much is okay. Then I focus on my breathing, as my teacher, Alondra, once taught me. Despite the blindfold, I close my eyes. My heart is thumping so hard and fast. I'm so nervous.

"Bye bye, Katie. Enjoy..."

17

MAGIC WITH A "K"

THE MINUTE ENORA PUTS THE BLINDFOLD ON, I WANT TO TAKE IT off. It's weird. I don't know how long I've had it on now because I can't tell time. But there's something about not being able to do something that gives you the urge to do it.

My whole body's shaking. I think maybe the shaking is from the alcohol? I don't know. I'm an easy drunk.

But...wait? I just had a sip.

I can't tell what's going on anymore. Or how long it's been.

But I keep hearing whispers. Thousands of whispers.

Aiwass. Aiwass. Aiwass.

I see lights, or flashes of light, of different colors. Is that the hallucination I'm supposed to be seeing? It's like rainbow colors and lights flashing everywhere in darkness. It reminds me of stars I've seen when I was sick, like when I'm nauseous and about to throw up and I see flashing lights by the sides of my head. You know, when you're dizzy looking up, and you see those flashes of light? Do you ever see those lights?

I feel stupid. Am I supposed to see something? All I see is blackness now. If anything, I feel sick. I mean, I guzzled down half a bottle of whiskey. Maybe I'm going to throw up... Or was it just a sip?

That's when I see light. It's almost welcoming after waiting to see anything for so long. It's a bird, not a raven, like wicked Enora, but a flaming, fiery bird, like a phoenix. And its fire is gliding slowly across a dark sky. I follow it with my eyes, watching it trail across infinite darkness as its multicolored tail blurs.

I'm on a street. Two people stand before one another shaking hands. One is in a bathing suit, dripping wet from a swimming pool. But the pool by his side is really a mirage—a false image of a small pool of water by a palm tree. The stranger was swimming along gravel. He was never in real water. It was just sand and rocks.

I see a black bird. But it's not just one bird. It is spinning another bird in its talons, circling around and around in darkness. There's no sun, just the light emanating from these birds.

Or am I in the woods?

I see stars above, through leaves and branches. The stars are so vivid and beautiful. It looks like the trees of Hawthorne Forest, the woods I love, back home. And the stars are so bright. But what awes me is not the light of the stars, but the darkness between them. It's the emptiness or blackness between the stars that entrances me. That's what is so beautiful. The blackness. That is numbness. And it is darkness again. It is the darkness that lights the night sky.

What am I doing? I feel stupid. I want to take this damn blindfold off.

"*Don't take it off,*" whispers Enora in my ear. "*Don't.*"

What is darkness? What is emptiness? What is a void? What is nothingness? Is that what I'm supposed to feel? Am I not supposed to see the light or the stars, or the birds, or the crickets, or the frogs croaking? Am I simply supposed to see what lies between it all? No light. No sound. Void. Nothingness. No *Cadence*?

Why did Enora tell me I needed someone by my side? I could have simply put on a blindfold alone.

A tunnel of light forms. My body is moving at a tremendous speed through it and I feel the air against my cheeks as my body pushes through the air. Lines of light from the tunnel speed past my eyes. Where am I being pulled to? I don't know. But at the end of the tunnel is nothing. That same darkness. The same thing I see within my blindfold. The same quiet I hear in my room. This darkness is the most wonderful feeling I've ever felt. That's my destination. It's calming. No one can ever take away a shadow. That's me now. I am a shadow. Like my Book of Shadows. I am completely nothing.

The tunnel spins faster. I see a thousand dark birds circle as my body jerks forward at an even more tremendous speed. But the darkness is now the brightest light I've ever seen.

Someone takes my hand. I'm not flying anymore. I'm spinning in circles with my feet twirling on a white marble dance floor. My partner is wearing a black suit and a small black bird mask with a hooked beak. He moves faster than any dancer I've ever seen, easily twirling me around and around. He beckons me on with his hand and his hips. I move with him.

Soon I find myself dancing with hundreds of men, all sharply dressed in the same attire. All of them have those same beak masks. But the ladies are wearing long white dresses and wear domino masks made of elegant white lace.

I'm pulled into a circle in the middle of all of them, then I'm dipped close to the granite floor amid their dance. The white ground shifts. Blurring.

I see distinctive stone statues along a terrace. They're lovely. Upon a wall I see monkeys playing violins. Their hairy hands move like virtuosos as we dance to their grand music. Hundreds of us. Thousands of us. We're in a ballroom, dancing around and around, and I'm just being led by the hand. Or a talon. And it feels wonderful.

Where is that fear I'm supposed to feel? I'm not afraid.

I feel nothing.

"Cadence?"

I look around in darkness. That wasn't Enora. That sounded like Bryce. It breaks my spell for a moment, and all I see is the darkness under the blindfold. I want to take it off.

"Don't take the blindfold off," Enora whispers.

"Yeah, Bryce? What?"

"Why are you dancing on a white tombstone?"

I nearly take the blindfold off over those strange words...but I don't. I remember my instructions.

There's a knock.

"Cadence?"

"I'm busy, Bryce."

"Cadence."

"Not now, okay?"

"What's going on in there? Can't you just unlock the door and let me in?"

"No, leave me alone."

I see a slowly rising sun. No, it's an eclipse on the horizon. Its yellow and white ring is so pretty that it makes my eyes tear. I reach up to wipe the tears, but then I feel the red silk over my eyes.

Someone grabs my hands and yanks them down, away from my face.

I see candles and my grimoire below me. I'm sitting in a chalk circle. I recognize a bed and nightstand. This is my guest room. It's as if I can see the room despite my eyes being covered.

"Cadence," says Maddie. "Did you know I was once a raven too?"

"Cadence!" shouts Bryce. "Open the door. What's going on in there?"

"I'm drinking."

He turns the knob and walks in.

My magic is growing. Is this dark magic? Its calming.

Bryce walks inside the room. He's staring down at me.

"What are you doing, babe?"

"Oh, my god, Bryce!" Maddie's right behind him. "She's cursed."

"Execrated," Bryce whispers. "Execrated."

Aiwass. Aiwass. Aiwass.

"What are you doing, Katie?"

Maddie reaches for my blindfold, but I bat her hand away.

"No!" cries Enora's voice. "Do not take the blindfold off, Windstorm!"

"Cadence!" Bryce sounds confused. He touches my hand. It feels electric, as if his hand is a bolt of energy. "Since I've met you, you've done everything to avoid this! This is black magic. Maddie was right. You are cursed."

"I know I am, Bryce."

He reaches over to touch my blindfold, but I lurch back. "Let me take this off you."

"Babe, this is what I was talking about," Maddie says, crying. "You're sick. A witch is casting a black magic spell on you."

"I know, Maddie. It's Enora. It feels wonderful."

Someone touches my shoulder. I think it's Maddie. She's crying.

"Babe, please let us help you," Maddie says.

"After the spell. I need to do this. Okay? For Hawthorne."

"Bryce, should we just pull the blindfold off?" Maddie asks.

"No! You mustn't take the blindfold off!"

∼

I'm crouching alone, naked, in pouring rain before a large white tombstone. The tombstone is nothing special; it's just a large block of white concrete. But it's white, alabaster white, a stone that, unlike all the crosses and tombs around me, seems to be so pure. It reminds me of the stone at the terrace, and the statues, and the dance floor in my vision.

Lying beside me in a bed with wet sheets is another woman, naked, crouched in a fetal position. Her back and butt, facing me, have been drenched by pouring rain. I recognize her face, I think. She's so clean from the rain. And her profile is almost youthful. She has long blond hair. Pale skin. She's shivering, but I don't think it's the cold. She looks so different, but I recognize her. She's Melanie, the Samhain Witch.

On my left, Enora is lying in the nude on another bed. All the sheets are wrinkled and soaked red. Enora's body is covered with bloody cuts again.

"I'm sick," I say. It's my lips but not my voice. "I'm dying."

Enora turns and gazes at me. She seems younger and doesn't have her familiar snide look. She's looking over, almost curious, with her bright sapphire eyes.

"The doctors say it's cancer, cancer of the womb. I leave this world for the Summerland soon, Raven."

"I will never forgive you."

"Your ritual begins now, Cadence."

I turn and see a dark-skinned man with a goatee. He is wearing a black suit with sunglasses and leaning on a cane. One of the lenses of his shades is missing. His head is tilted down, so I can't see his face, but he gestures for me to follow him. I feel as if death itself has arrived. He points his cane up the hill, covered in wild grass, toward a white manor. I recognize it. It's the house from my dream. The house by Loch Ness.

I look down, and I'm naked.

He leads me, twirling his cane, to the front door. Inside I hear drums, and I see flickering firelight again.

We walk down a narrow hallway. I pass that same shadowed kitchen in ruins. Then we enter a living room lit by torches and candles.

There are bloodstains on the ground. They seem more dark than red in the flickering light. Dancers, over twenty of them now, crowd the central room, twirling in some kind of trance. All of them are naked and wet, as if drenched by rain. But all of them are wearing domino masks—the men have black beak masks and the women have beaked white lace ones. Some men spin in a frenzy. The only one not dancing is the man in the dark suit with a cane. When he finally turns, I recognize this dark-skinned man. Aamon.

Aamon walks over to a central altar beside the chimney. Once more, like in my dream, the altar has a black flag with a red backward pentagram, crosses, and a large skull with horns. There are instruments on another table beside it. I see a silvery hook, knives, and even a small silver saw, reminding me of surgical tools—or instruments of torture.

Aamon raises a golden chalice to the sky with both hands. He drinks from it. Then he wipes the edges of the chalice with a white cloth from the table.

He gestures for me to sit on the throne once more.

All the dancers crowding the room twirl crazily under me, as if they're putting on a play. Four torchbearers stand motionless, one in each corner of the hall.

Something about the naked dancers seems wrong. It doesn't even feel lewd. Their dancing seems jerky and unnatural. Many stare up at the ceiling with wide eyes as if drugged. The frenzied dance reminds me of voodoo trances I've studied. In fact, in the center, one of the ladies cuts the throat of a chicken. Blood drips down her breasts, and it seems to only send her into more of a frenzy, shaking on the floor.

"Drink," Aamon says calmly with a grin, holding the chalice before me.

Two ladies stand beside him and nod. "Drink and you will be reborn," the girls say in unison.

I shake my head.

The ladies both hold the golden chalice and raise it before me.

"*Choronzon, mighty god,*" they say, beside Aamon, in unison. "*Choronzon, reveal thyself to this vessel. Unveil shadows. Show darkness within light. Lux tenebris. Lux tenebris.*"

"Drink," repeats Aamon with a nod.

I take the chalice in shaky hands.

"You deserve it, Alondra," Enora says bitterly. She's lying on the bed again, bloody, facing me. "I really hope you die."

All turns bright and I'm back in the room with all the frenzied dancing. The drums beat faster. And all I smell is bodies: human sweat and bodies.

Alondra appears, standing in the place of Aamon. She is wearing a dark cloak, but she is naked underneath.

"Drink, Cadence," Alondra says with a reassuring smile, bringing the chalice close to my lips. "Drink and you'll feel reborn. Feel darkness within light. Gnosis. Our understanding of everything. We gift that to you. Just like the garden. We gift gnosis, Windstorm."

"I want to be good," I say, shaking my head.

"There is no good," Alondra says. "I've told you before.

When you see darkness between light, the moon upon the sun, you shall have gnosis. You are a witch. A High Priestess of the Hawthorne coven. You must see beyond this world."

"No."

I push the cup away.

But Alondra doesn't relent. She pushes the chalice to my lips again. "Drink and understand."

"No," I say, shaking my head. "Why didn't you show me all this before, Alondra? Melanie seems peaceful enough. She's just resting in peace by her grave now."

"Hawthorne is in peril until you see what I see."

"You keep saying it's in trouble, but you won't tell me how or why."

"I can't tell you. I can only show you."

A shadow is cast over Alondra. I look to my left and see a dark-skinned woman in a white headdress and a white dress. This is my ancestor Escoba, standing behind her. And she looks mad.

"Quick, Cadence," Alondra says nervously, glancing over her shoulder, "There's no time. Drink now."

"What's in it?"

"Goat's blood. Wine. And semen."

There's a scream. All the dancers back away from the center of the room, where, in a red circle and pentagram, lies Enora. She's bloodied again, now writhing and shaking in pain, screaming as if being stabbed over and over by some shadowy figure. It's horrible. But most horrible, amid all the dancers, no one's helping her. After Enora wails a few more times, the dancers dance and twirl over her, smiling and laughing, ignoring all her pain.

And then...I see nothing.

~

"Katie?" The voice seems so far away.

It seems like it could be miles away. It's so quiet. But so sweet. I recognize the accent. I feel tears rush into my eyes. It's Frida.

"Katie?" Frida asks in a whisper. "Please, Katie, come back to us. Come back."

"I'm sick, Frida," I say, shaking my head. "I have cancer of the womb."

I feel a hand touch mine. Again, my senses are so heightened that the touch is electrifying.

"Katie? Please, Katie—" Frida's crying. "Please come back. I'm sorry. Please come back, Cadence. We love you."

"But I can't see, Frida. I can't see anymore."

"Sweetie, come back home."

That's my mom's voice—my mom who passed away a few years ago. That voice is so sweet and sounds so real. Oh, I miss her so much!

I feel another touch on my hand. Again, every touch is like a bolt of lightning in the nothingness, made stronger by having my eyes covered.

"I can't see, Mom. I can't see!"

But I hear.

All of a sudden, I hear the ringing of a thousand bells rush to my ears. It's like the time we fought the Samhain Witch and I cast that evil satanic spell to save Liam. The peal of some of the bells is tinny, some baritone. But all are loud, like church bells. And then...

"It is done," Enora's voice says. "The spell is cast. You may remove your blindfold, initiate."

I pull off my blindfold.

There's nothing special before me. Enora is on her knees,

picking up all the candles and tossing them in her large red bag.

"Till we meet again, in one week in Alabama, Windstorm," Enora says. Then she walks away, heading back to the trees. "I'm gonna hurt that witch, I'm going to hurt her real good now, with your infernal help. Remember, you owe me. Until then, bye bye."

She slings the bag over her shoulder. The field lights are still on, and they seem so bright to my open eyes.

"Is it done?" I holler, still on my knees. "Is it over?"

"You're free," she says, without turning back.

I watch her disappear into the trees. Then I sit alone in the center of the grassy field.

Soon, a brilliant light rises through the trees. It's so bright that I squint. I quickly turn from it. Usually, I welcome the sunrise. This morning it feels stale. Cold. I don't yearn for light. I want to feel that numbness again. That calm in darkness. I want to feel that. And... no, I just want to go home. I want to sleep.

18

FRIGID BURNING

I'm standing in the tall grass in my glade, in bare feet, wearing only a black lace nightgown. I think it's noon?

I feel so tired.

I feel so cold.

I wrap my arms around my body. Is this the dark magic I'm supposed to feel now? I extend my hands over my violet bonfire, but the flames are just not warm enough.

I feel awful.

I threw up in the bathroom twice before I came out into the backyard.

"Cadence," says a voice quietly behind me.

I'd recognize that voice anywhere. It's my best friend, Madison. I turn. She's cautiously approaching me wearing a black T-shirt and white shorts. Her face is decked out in goth makeup, but with the shorts, it looks like she could go for a summer picnic. Isn't she freezing?

I turn back, rubbing my hands over the purple flames.

"Frida will be all right," Maddie says. "It's my fault. I asked for her to come and help you. Just forget it."

"What are you talking about?"

"You yelled at her when you came home."

I did? I don't remember that. I don't even remember coming home.

But I remember the spell. I remember every weird thing that happened vividly. I think I heard Frida in my vision? I definitely don't remember yelling at her.

Wasn't the dark magic supposed to rid me of my curse? Or is this the cold remnants of Enora's spell? It would have been nice for Enora to have told me what else to expect.

"I partook in a devil ceremony, Maddie. I've got enough things on my mind right now." I dip down, rub my hands together, and put them closer to the flames. "How are you?"

"Better than you, I think. Babe, I think you're under a witch curse."

"I know I'm under a curse. You worried about this even back when we were in New York. And I told you I just partook in a black magic spell. Enora's spell. I'm trying to be better, Maddie."

"Enora? Why would you cast a spell with Enora?" She sounds angry. "That's why Bryce and I went nuts when you got home, Cadence. That's why Frida cried. We just don't understand why you would ever do that."

"I don't care." I blow into my hands. It's so cold. Then I squint up at the clear sky.

"You're acting exactly like I did when I was cursed last year," Maddie says. "And—" her voice starts cracking. "You got me through all that, Kates."

Her crying hurts. I don't want to feel pain. I don't want to feel anything. I love Madison so much, just like I love Frida, but I don't want to feel anything anymore. I want to feel numb.

"Just leave me alone. You guys want me to lead our coven? Then why don't you leave me alone?"

She hesitantly touches my shoulder, barely and so gently, with her fingertips.

"I care too much to ever leave you, Cadence. I called Liam. Bryce told me a week ago you'd been acting so weird, like a vampire, sleeping all day and staying up all night. But the noises were worrying him the most. Every night he heard horrible screams from downstairs. At first, he told me he didn't even believe it was you. He said every night you scream, waking him up. Not to mention, you were supposed to lecture. But forget that. Bryce and the rest of us are just worried. So is Mom. And so is your dad."

"*Dad shouldn't be with your mom!*"

"I know. I know," Maddie says, raising her hand. "Forget that, Katie. I'm not trying to get you upset. I'm here for you. Don't think about—"

But my whole body starts violently shaking. Is it rage or the cold? It's so cold. My teeth chatter. My body shakes. I'm back to rubbing my hands close to the flames, but it's not doing any good. *It's so damn cold!*

The ground seems to move. The trees swoon, coming closer to me, and then far. My head aches. I see flashes of light in my periphery, like when I had the blindfold on. But it's not pleasant. I feel sick. I dip down and...throw up.

Maddie gently touches my back.

"It's okay, Cadence."

"Maddie, please go away from me," I say softly. My voice breaks, fighting tears. "Just stay away from me, Maddie."

"Why did you do this spell, babe? Liam told me you shouldn't have."

"Alondra told me to."

"Bryce told me he heard Alondra say that. But even if it was Alondra, Cadence, even if she were still alive, she would never have wanted you to do it. I, all of us in the circle, don't get it. She didn't teach you this kind of magic because *you* stopped her from teaching it, Cadence."

"Honestly, Maddie—" I feel tears finally streaming down

my face. I pause, but my voice isn't breaking. I'm too upset to cry now, I suppose. "I think it might have been the worst thing I've ever done in my life. I don't even know if I trust Alondra anymore. But then, I don't know who I can trust. I think I've changed."

She gently rubs my back. And from behind, I hear her start crying too.

I get on my knees and lean close to the fire, so close that I practically touch the flames with my fingers. It's still cold, but warmer. Oddly, I find that the tips of my fingers can pass through the purple flames without burning.

I shiver again.

"What are you doing, Cadence?"

"Trying to warm my hands by the fire. It's just so cold."

"There's no fire from those logs."

"There's purple flames here."

"There's nothing but a pile of wood."

I look up at the sun. It's eclipsed. But it's not dark. It's brighter than the eclipse we watched here two years ago. There's a clear blue sky, almost summer, amidst the ring of light. Have I lost my mind? An eclipse? How? And a purple bonfire that doesn't exist?

That's it. I break down and finally cry. Like really cry. Like with tears flowing harder than ever. I'm on my knees, and I just fucking cry so hard. And it's really bad because Maddie...who loves me so much...she loses it beside me. But I don't want to cry! Crying only brings in all those feelings that hurt.

I feel her put an arm over me. I hate crying, but what else am I supposed to do? So...we kneel with our arms around each other and just cry.

"It's okay, babe," Maddie says. "All of us are so worried. All your friends and family care so much about you. That's why we're all here at the house."

I nod.

"Cadence, it's a curse," she says between tears. "It's not just you and Bryce and Frida. You know I flipped last year because of Enora, but, babe...I told you, you're the one who brought me back. You came to Enora's house. You risked everything to save me, Kates. Just like you helped Alondra. You've helped everyone. But now...why would you cast a spell with Enora?" She pauses, fighting back tears again. "Forget that. What can I do to help you?"

"Nothing. It's too late for me."

"Maybe Liam can help?"

"He killed a little girl, Maddie," I say, shaking my head. I rub my eyes with the back of my nightgown sleeve. "That's why he doesn't cast magic anymore. I can't trust anyone. Except you... and Bryce. I still love him so much, but I can't tell him. I'm, I'm just so worried everyone will abandon me. I'm so scared, Maddie."

"He knows, Cadence. He loves you."

"Can Frida forgive me?"

"She's having a hard enough time forgiving herself. She feels so horrible. She feels responsible, Cadence. She heard a mouthful from me already. That's why she came to the house today. We think she was the catalyst for you going bonkers." She backs up and raises a hand. "Now, don't get upset over my calling you bonkers, Cadence. That and your letter did this. Or maybe it was your dad and Mom? I don't know. But now, don't be getting mad about that either."

"Stop worrying I'm going to get mad."

"You kinda are mad, babe. Sorry. Anyway, I yelled like crazy at poor Frida right after you did—just for different reasons. So when you snapped at her today, you weren't the only one yelling at her, she's been hearing it from me and yelling at herself."

"I don't want her to feel bad. I don't even recall yelling at her. I don't even remember coming home."

"You did."

I try to get up, but the trees spin. Maddie helps me stand.

"I love Frida so much, Maddie. Alondra lost Jane because of her dark magic. Then she lost Liam. I think that connection with Alondra's friends made me lose it when Frida said she didn't want to talk to me again. Just tell her I'm sorry."

"Why don't you tell her yourself?" She helps me stand straight. "Everything's going to be fine. Nothing's changed. Just this freak spell. I spoke to Liam. He said he's done that same blindfold voodoo spell a few times. He says it hasn't damned you. You're still good, babe."

"How many evil spells do I have to cast before you guys stop saying I'm good?"

"A lot, I think," Maddie says with a shrug. "You're too good a person, Cadence."

"Maddie... I feel cold. I feel really cold."

Maddie puts her arms around me again.

19

LESS ELUSIVE ELEUSINIAN

I'M WEARING SHADES, CARRYING MY HEAVY LEATHER BAG SLUNG over my shoulder, rushing through the corridors of two buildings on my way to a trailer classroom. It's hot as hell, and my flaxen yellow T-shirt is drenched. I'm huffing and puffing because I'm totally out of shape—and I'm totally late. My heavy bag isn't helping. I have a final exam. It's an advanced class on Alexander the Great. I've missed nearly half of the discussion groups, and, based on the letter from Dr. Brainer, you can probably guess how bad my grades are. But our final grade is based on this exam.

I walk up a few steps and open the thin metal door to the trailer. Eight people are sitting around the table looking nervous as hell, and our professor, old Dr. Stoferson, is at the center of the table passing everyone a sheet of paper.

Dr. Stoferson is the nicest professor at Hawthorne University. (No, actually, he's probably the nicest professor in the world.) I was in his Civil War class last year with Tammy. Had this year been "normal," this probably would have been my favorite class. Dr. Stoferson doesn't have to teach, he's way beyond retirement, he just loves his job that much.

"Mrs. Cadence Wallace," he says as I walk inside, "so nice of you to join us all for your final exam."

"Sorry."

He hands me a blank sheet of paper with a tremulous hand. And only Dr. Stoferson could flash me a smile and genuinely not look angry.

"Sorry," I say again, sitting down at the only empty seat.

Across from me is a fellow classmate I know well. Frida. She looks down sadly, averting her eyes.

"Now that all of you have a blank sheet of paper..." Dr. Stoferson says slowly. Then he pauses. The man is so frail it looks like it's a chore to speak. But he flashes me a grin again. "Now that you have it, you may prepare for our impromptu exam. You will not be graded on what you write but on what you say this morning. Use your page as notes. Gather information on something we've discussed over the past few months. Then when you're called on, you'll have five minutes to discuss this topic, which you've independently drawn from your own thoughts. If you've been in class—" He annoyingly looks over at me. "You might have already prepared some ideas after all my hints. If not? I want you each to come up with something unique. This is an advanced class. Don't discuss something I can read in a book. With all the talking we've done, you should be able to come up with something, or at least modify something we've discussed. You have ten minutes to write notes and then use what you've written for the discussion."

He removes his glasses, types something on his laptop, and nods.

And then I stare at a blank sheet of paper...

Fuck.

What am I going to come up with? I haven't spoken about anything in class because I keep ditching all his classes. But I have read a ton of books on Alexander the Great...

My pen starts practically moving by itself. Is that you, Alondra? No, it's my handwriting.

Aristotle and the Eleusinian mysteries... Aristotle was... likely initiated. The mysteries involved the secret cult in ancient Greece and Macedonia worshipping Persephone.

Three major cycles: Descent, search and ascent.

Isn't it fascinating that this corresponds quite remarkably with the Celtic mystic trinity of life: the maiden, the mother, the crone? The trinity celebrated in Beltane with the Green Man? Is there a connection? Certainly both were ancient agrarian practices.

I put my pen down, lean back in my plastic chair, and wait. I'm done. Dr. Stoferson looks up at me and furrows his brow. Because it's only been a minute.

I look over at Frida. She's staring at a blank page. Part of me wants to dismiss this final, walk around the table, and throw my arms around her. Maybe hand her my notes? I'm so sorry for how I treated her. I'm so sorry.

My gaze turns to the window. Beyond the tree-lined path to the trailer are clear skies. This is one of my favorite classrooms because it's out on the very edge of campus, completely enveloped by the wilderness. That's probably why Dr. Stoferson loves it too. But it's hot. Fortunately, the trailer is air conditioned. Still, sweat is dripping down my back because I rushed to class late.

Dr. Stoferson is curious as hell over what I've written. He

keeps furrowing his brow and trying to look over and take a peek. Most of the students haven't jotted anything down yet.

Frida's still writing. She looks up for a moment, and her eyes accidentally land right on my eyes.

"*I'm so sorry*," I mouth.

She nods. She doesn't look angry. She just looks sad.

Then she's back to writing.

I stare down at what I wrote. Is it enough? It's an interesting theory, one that definitely will impress Dr. Stoferson as unique. I think? Did they discuss this connection? Should I add more? But we only have a minute or two until our discussion, and I'll say more when I start yapping.

After sitting and staring at the trees, Dr. Stoferson finally coughs and claps his hands.

"That's enough time. Cadence, you wrote your notes first, what aspect of Hellenism and Alexander do you want to discuss?"

"Aristotle," I say with a nod. "I'm fascinated by philosophy in ancient Greece, Dr. Stoferson—philosophy that would have been taught to Alexander the Great, helping the general deal with his fears of death in battle. After all, Aristotle taught the emperor. Is his teacher, Aristotle, an okay topic to cover?"

Dr. Stoferson nods.

"Well, Aristotle taught Alexander, guys. But Aristotle was taught by Plato. And Plato was, of course, taught by Socrates. Anyway, Aristotle claimed to have learned *mysteries*. It's very possible that he was involved in the Eleusinian mysteries— maybe taking hallucinogenic ergot, maybe not? All of us here know that these mysteries involved three phases of life: descent, search, and ascent. The descent represented Persephone's rape and abduction. The search had to do with her mother's sorrow over the loss of her daughter. The ascent had to do with her return to Earth. All of this represents two things symbolically:

the seasons on Earth and—this is the connection I'm about to explain—the life cycle of a woman.

"Now we just had our Beltane ceremony on May first. Some of you might have attended on the grounds of the Billington house, or former house. I was there. It was fabs." A few students snicker. Frida smiles but looks away. "Isn't it interesting that in Celtic traditions, the May Queen is a triple goddess made up of three stages: the maiden, the mother, and the crone. Each stage represents a time in a lady's life. Her early life where she is the maiden, fertile, exploring the world, like Persephone in her fields. The next is her middle stage, as a mother. And finally as an old woman. The three stages of life.

"So I'm proposing that these three stages are one and the same as the Eleusinian mysteries. Like Persephone, the woman roams her fields—she's fertile. She marries (though she was raped in the story because women were treated like complete trash back in ancient Greece). Finally Persephone returns to the earth. Reborn? Reincarnated? Perhaps that's the whole mystery in the ancient ritual?

"Anyway, these three parts, a trinity seen over and over in so many traditions in our world, represent youth, midlife, and death, or spring, fall, and winter. It's the life cycle of a woman coupled with the life of our planet. In an agrarian society, it gives meaning to people's lives. Just like the Celtic tradition gives meaning to a witch's life. So...I'm positing that both of these traditions are one and the same."

One of the students tosses his pen hard on the table and heaves a sigh. Dr. Stoferson has a really large smile. Frida is staring at the table, but I see the hint of a grin on her face.

20

I'M LEAVING

"*Lux alba*. Blessings come from Hecate. Glory be the stars. Let not a cloud block Selene. And if it be, let the rays of light come forth in the morrow. Blessed be our Hawthorne coven under our gods Gaia, Selene, and Astraeus. *Lux tenebris*. Blessed be. May you never thirst."

"*Yatu*, witches."

"*Yatu*," they all echo.

This sabbath in my backyard is long overdue. We haven't met for weeks. Of course, Frida didn't show up, which is no surprise. What is a surprise is that Bryce is sitting across from me in a black robe. After our nuclear war—that anniversary dinner—and after not talking to one another over the past week, I figured there was no way he'd show up. I'm avoiding his eyes.

"As I draw down the moon, do not forget the peace in our circle, sisters." I rise, lift my arms up toward the quarter moon, close my eyes, and focus on the white rays of light.

Then I sit back down.

"Frida's not joining us?" Mandy asks in her Southern accent. The bitch is starting early, apparently.

"She couldn't make it," Bryce says.

Normally, Mandy or Natasha would now go full-on berserko, saying something nastier to me, but I think there's something about my expression that shuts her up.

"We should be grateful for those who are here," I say.

"Hey, did you guys hear about Tammy?" asks shy Helen.

"Duh, Helen," says Maddie, rolling her eyes.

"I'm so happy for her," Josie chimes in. "Apparently Nathan's got his pilot's license. They're flying to Jamaica for their marriage. She told me she wants to incorporate a hand-fasting, but Nathan is not a witch. So she's not sure if it will be with a priest or a High Priest."

"I'm so happy for her too," Helen says.

"Destination weddings are fun," Maddie says. "And they can be less expensive because, you know, you don't have to invite too many people." She laughs. "Except us. If we get married, we'll have to invite our whole crew from this circle." She turns to my brother and says, "If *I* had a wedding, *I'd* have it here in Katie and Bryce's yard. Just like Kate's. Speaking of weddings, Damie..."

"Cut it out, Maddie," I say.

"Don't worry, no plans yet, sis," Damie quickly says.

"Says you, handsome," Maddie adds, touching his hand. "Says you."

Then it gets real quiet again. Too quiet.

"I've got two important matters to discuss tonight," I say. "First is our coven. Many of you are leaving by Litha. Maybe, if you're close by, like in Atlanta or Savannah, you can still come Fridays? Hope so. But basically, I'm looking for you guys' help in recruiting. Any friends or neighbors around town, anybody into magic or the occult, let me know. The circle is going to be incomplete."

"The circle is already incomplete," quips Mandy.

"Mandy, no," snaps Maddie, shaking her head adamantly. Maddie turns to me, looking nervous.

"Everything is open for discussion," says Natasha, shaking her head. "Windstorm has always valued openness. We all know she's fighting with everybody. She's gone crazy. Why fight Frida, Cadence? Why would anyone fight Frida, the nicest girl in the world? Most of us are on her side. Bryce, you're fighting with the High Priestess too, right?"

"Our High Priestess has been execrated," Mandy says with a nod. "Only she wasn't hurt physically, she's just plain gone nuts."

"Can you guys try to not be bitches for once tonight?" Maddie says.

"It's okay," I say with a chuckle. "I have gone mad, Madds. I'm not hiding it. You guys wanted to meet, so I'm here. Anyway, that's the second issue. Execration."

I pause and throw my dark hair back with a sigh. I know this next thing is going to make them go ballistic.

"Is Alondra inside you now?" Debra interjects shyly to my left. "I never knew her, but that possession could have a huge thing to do with your curse. Maybe you just need to get rid of her spirit, like Kenosha and Agnes tried to do?"

"Frida's not only afraid of black magic, she's afraid you're changing, Cadence," Josie interjects. "Sorry, but this is not just an execration. Cadence, because I love you, I'm gonna be honest with you. Many of us are thinking, you know, maybe you're not just possessed by Alondra, maybe you're becoming her. Maybe all this is Alondra."

"I don't think so," Bryce says, folding his arms. "I think she's under the Samhain Witch's curse."

"But you guys destroyed her home," says Damie.

"The only other evil witch that could curse Katie is Enora," Bryce says. "But why would Enora injure herself?"

"Alondra was evil, Bryce," Maddie says, shaking her head.

"It could be Alondra's spirit inside of Cadence causing her harm. Alondra hurt all of us. Maybe not directly, but Reardon did. It could be Alondra, even if it's her spirit inside Katie."

"Let's just cut the shit and ask her," snaps Mandy. "Why did you perform a dark voodoo spell, Cadence? Huh? You've instructed this circle a million times not to perform black magic. Why'd you do it? Rumor has it, it was actually shown to you by Enora. That means you were with her. Enora wanted all of us dead, if you remember."

"That's why we're meeting, Mandy," says Damie. "To help her."

"And why are you even fucking here?" Mandy snaps. "You're not initiated. Come here just because you're dating Blackbird? Or is it because you're the High Priestess's brother? Well, that doesn't make you—"

"Really, Mandy!" cries Maddie, getting up. "Shut the fuck up already!"

"Guys, please, calm down," says Bryce.

"It's a little too late to be calm, isn't it, Bryce?" asks Mandy. "Cadence should have consulted with us first, but she already went out and casted this evil spell. That endangers all of us. She doesn't care to be open anymore. Maddie, you told me you guys found Cadence in the guest room sitting on a red star—exactly what you were doing when you were cursed. Cadence, you said time and time again how fearful you were that you had already been cursed after you spoke that incantation against the Samhain Witch to free Liam. You warned each and every one of us. Why would you perform dark magic after—"

"She's cursed, stupid!" snaps Maddie. "Okay? That's why. That's why we're all here tonight!"

"I'm talking to her," Mandy says.

"Did you ask Kenosha?" Natasha asks Bryce. "She wanted to get Alondra out of Cadence." Natasha turns to me. "Or what about the spirit inside you?"

"Katie and I think that Alondra's spirit is a positive force," Bryce answers.

"High Priestess," Mandy says, "we came here to meet with each other in ceremony. Here we are. Now what can we do to fix this?"

"Come with me to Alabama," I reply with a sigh. "I plan to join Enora and fight Melanie."

Everybody goes absolutely nuts. I knew they would. This is why I've been so quiet. Even Bryce has completely lost his mind. I think I'm the only one still sitting down.

"*You're going to get us killed!*" Mandy yells.

"*You want to go back there?*" shouts Maddie. "*Cadence, with Enora?!*"

"Cadence," says Josie, shaking her head over and over, "Cadence, you met with us last year to plan our attack on Enora."

"No," Bryce snaps. "No, Cadence! You can't go back there. I forbid it. Not again. Especially with Enora. I won't allow this."

"Guys, I've been talking to Enora," I say, "because I think—"

"How did she even get out of jail?" asks Natasha.

"That's why we need her help," I reply with a nod. "She's the only one powerful enough. She performed a dark spell with me in Woodland Park in Hawthorne to prepare."

"How have you even been talking to her?" asks Damie.

"She's out of prison. And I have her cell number."

"*How the fuck do you have her phone number!*" snaps Mandy.

"I've been planning this for a while now," I say. "Enora knows I'm execrated. So is she. She suggested the blindfold spell to empower me. Enora and I are going to work together in Alabama to finally stop the Samhain Witch. That's the plan. Even Alondra's spirit suggested it. I agree. Sorry, guys, I agree."

I look over the flames at Bryce. He shakes his head like crazy.

"I don't agree with Kenosha."

"But you can't trust her, Cadence!" Bryce shouts. "We met with Enora to fight Reardon. She killed him and then tried to kill us!"

"She's flipped her lid!" says Natasha. "That's it. Talk about cursed. You want us to go back to that witch again? None of us are going to do that. Every time you go there, you barely get out alive."

"Do whatever the hell you want!" I shout, finally jumping up. "I believe our power grows when we stick together, but if you don't want to accompany me, I'll go alone."

"But Cadence," Maddie says. Her eyes are tearing up. She tugs at my arm to sit, but I yank it back. "Babe, not only do I think this is wrong, I'm afraid for you."

"Don't go with me then, Maddie," I say with a shrug. "Stay back again. I don't care."

"You're not going," Bryce says. "Not this time. I can't let you."

"How dare you! I'll do whatever the hell I want, Bryce. You might be my husband but I'm my own woman. Just because we're married doesn't mean you can order me around."

"You're not thinking straight," snaps Mandy.

"She's cursed," objects Maddie, wiping her eyes with the back of her hand.

"You're not going," Bryce insists.

"Look, I knew you guys wouldn't follow me," I say. "Many of you haven't wanted to follow me since Alondra died. I get it. I make a lousy leader. But you all wanted to meet and talk. So I did. You're scared, Maddie? You don't think I'm scared? You don't trust Enora? You think I trust her? I get that you don't want to go. Enora doesn't expect anyone from her coven to join her either. All the witches fear that witch."

"Then why are *you* going, Cadence?" snaps Bryce. "Three leading witches couldn't hold their own against her. Three of the most powerful witches in the world."

"You want to fight, Bryce? Why not fight with me *after* ceremony, away from my sisters. Why'd you even come here tonight?"

"I'm not only your husband, I'm your warlock for this coven. I'm your High Priest and this is the sabbath."

"Well, if you all are really a part of my coven, join me then."

"Katie," Damie says, "this is your hex talking."

"Shut up, Damie! Mandy's right, you shouldn't even be here!"

"But Enora, Cadence?" Maddie asks. "Enora? You're not thinking straight, babe. After everything we went through, why would you join *Enora*?"

"Fuck! Fine! Guys, do whatever the hell you want! There's no point in going round and round about this."

"When are you leaving?" Bryce asks, rubbing his eyes.

"What! Why? You plan to lock me up so I can't go?"

"When, Cadence?" Bryce asks with a sigh.

"Fuck off, Bryce. You and anyone else who's afraid, stay home. Married to you or not, I don't need a man telling me what to do. If you don't like it, why'd you marry a witch?"

"He just cares about you, Katie," Maddie says quietly, still wiping away tears. "He doesn't want anything bad to happen to you. Cadence, please, I told you about these curses. You can't go with Enora. You can't fight us, you need us together to—"

"I'm not fighting, Maddie. I'm simply leaving."

And after saying that, I turn and head back to my house.

All my friends murmur like crazy behind my back. In the past, I'd cry. I don't fucking cry anymore. I'm just really mad. If anything, I feel like I should make them feel as shitty as they just made me feel.

They think I'm a loon. Do you? There's a witch hunting us. None of the head witches of the council knows how to fight her, especially Kenosha. This witch has killed a sweet old lady, caused Willow to become disabled, defeated three of the most powerful witches in the world, and fucked with my head. So I'm going to work with Enora to stop her. So? What's the problem here?

"Come back, Cadence!" Maddie says in tears.

I show her my middle finger. Then, as I approach my patio, just for a little added theatrical effect, I close my eyes, clench a fist, and will our bonfire to blow out.

21

UN-EXPECTING NEWS

I'M TRYING TO BREATHE, SUFFOCATING AND SPITTING UP FILTH, dizzy enough to nearly pass out. My throat hurts. I feel so dizzy. I wipe my lips with the back of my hand. Some of my black lipstick stains my skin. I'm so sick. It's weird because I felt fine going to sleep, but I woke up nauseous and ran to the guest bathroom to throw up. I hate throwing up, it feels so horrible.

The toilet seat is swerving.

I cough and spit up more phlegm. Then I feel a cramp in my belly.

"Are you all right, Cadence?" Bryce asks, knocking on the door.

No. I'm not all right.

The timer I set in our bathroom goes off. I either ate something real bad or... I scramble to stand up and look at the test on the counter. I feel so unsteady.

"Cadence?" Bryce asks, knocking again. "Are you okay?"

I lean over the counter. There are two lines in the window of the plastic thingy. According to the box, one line means not pregnant, but two lines means—"

"Cadence!"

"*What! I'm fine, Bryce. Okay? Just go away!*"

"I heard you throwing up."

"Just go back to your studying."

I kneel over the toilet again.

"It's four in the morning," he says.

I'm pregnant? WTF?

Guess that explains why I missed my period last month.

"Why don't you come upstairs and go to bed?" Bryce asks. The door is still locked.

"Because we're fighting."

"It's fine, Cadence. Just forget it. Just forget everything. It's all my fault. We can—"

"Fight later? About money or curfews?"

I'm pregnant? Are you kidding me?

Aren't I supposed to be happy? I've been dreaming of this all my life. I feel like shit. Maybe the test is wrong? It's a good thing I didn't drink during Enora's spell. Hey, maybe that's why I was vomiting?

"I must have eaten something bad," I lie. "Just go back to bed, Bryce."

"Can you unlock the door, please?"

"Nope. I'm still mad at you. You're a controlling, chauvinistic jerk."

"Well," he snaps, "maybe at least this will stop you from going on another road trip tomorrow alone."

"Nope. Still going."

I'm pregnant!?... Yippee.

Looks like Bryce and I are going to make fantastic parents, fighting like crazy all the time. I rub my belly. Chandra, look forward to a split-personality witch-mom and a pesky, overprotective warlock-dad.

"I'll be home from the office by four tomorrow," he hollers outside the door. "I can drive you to Alabama after."

I answer by throwing up in the toilet again. Then there's more incessant knocking on the door.

"*Scram, Bryce! Just go away!*"

22

BLACK WAND

I stop my Jaguar at the end of a dirt road by a clearing in the forest. This clearing used to have a creepy broken-down house. Not anymore. Now there's just a large dead field. It's weird because there's not even a sign of the house, no walls or debris. It's just an empty field of tree trunks, dead bushes, and wild grass. This is creepy. My witches and I were inside this house the day after Halloween. And Liam was *inside* the house before I made it disappear. So why is there not even a roof shingle or piece of a wall? Was it ever here?

The wild grassy glade, surrounded by all the trees of Geneva Forest, goes on for a couple miles. And in the far distance, I see a heavyset witch in a pitch-black cloak traipsing slowly around the dead shrubs. She's holding a book under her arm, and she keeps reaching down and picking up dead weeds, grass, and dirt, but I can't make out her face from this distance.

I park behind two cars on the dirt road: a plain red car with an Indiana license plate and a large gray SUV. As I open my door, that bitch Enora gets out of her large gray SUV. She's wearing a long draping black blouse with a large lace collar and slacks.

"Panthera," I say, getting out of my car.

"Hi, Katie," Enora says, with her back to me. She pulls out a small black book and wand from her passenger seat. "Ready to kick some witch-ass?" She turns and gazes at me with her pretty blue eyes. She has a snake and upside-down cross penciled on her forehead—she's always pretty in her loathsome wickedness. "Where's your robe?"

"In the back seat. Who's that?" I point to the witch in the field.

Enora squints. "Just another raven," she replies with a smirk.

"Huh?"

"Mira."

"Mira?"

It is Mira! I finally recognize her as she walks closer to us.

"How sweet," Enora says, rolling her eyes. "I wonder who else might show up for a reunion?"

I put my black robe on over my T-shirt and jeans. Mira is close enough to be waving now.

"Can't find her, Cadence," Mira shouts. "There's no one here. I don't even see any sign of the ruins of her house. Everything's disappeared. It's just an empty field. I don't see that witch anywhere."

"She's here," Enora says, looking around the surrounding forest.

"But I see a degenerate bitch accompanying you," quips Mira.

"Greetings from Hecate to you too, Mira," Enora answers. "Blessed be."

Mira probably hears her, but she's doing her very best to ignore her. As she comes closer, I can make out the demon tattoos along Mira's neck. Then, when she is even closer, I see the horizontal scar on her neck—the scar made by the witch standing beside me, who once cut her throat. Mira probably hates Enora more than anyone.

"You're crazy, you know that, Cadence," Mira says, embracing me. "I couldn't get why you're working with Enora until Maddie told me about the curse. I planned my trip a while back, but when I heard about *her* joining you—" Mira scowls at Enora. "I quickly booked an earlier flight. The mere fact that you're talking to her tells me you're under a spell."

"Missed you too, Raven." Enora scowls, scrunching her nose.

"Yeah, well, I flew by plane and then rented a car. The council approves. They've sent me. Willow is still too sick. Aurora and Olwyn don't mind this confrontation. They'd be here if it weren't for the fact that they're so far away."

"Oh, so you're a part of their stupid so-called council now, too?" asks Enora with a laugh. "Figures."

"Yes, Panthera," Mira says, "I'm also here to watch you. Spying is something you enjoy so much. Not only are you in trouble with the law, you're in trouble with us."

Enora laughs.

"But, guys, the trouble is I can't find her." She stares back at the field. "I've been searching for the past hour, scouring the field for the witch."

"How's your neck?" asks Enora.

"Stop it, Enora," I snap. "We need to stick together."

"But not with her," Enora objects. "I said I needed *you* to meet me, Cadence. I need *your* magic, not a weak witch like her. The plan was for me to trap Melanie and for you to finish her off using what I taught you."

"We already destroyed her home," Mira says.

"We're going to stop her once and for all," I say, shaking my head.

"How?" asks Mira. "Do you plan to kill her?"

"Would that be allowed by your illustrious *council*, Raven?" Enora says.

"She almost killed Enora, Mira," I say.

"She deserves it, Cadence. Perhaps we should ask her why she was attacked?"

"I don't know why the bitch attacked me," Enora replies. "All I know is she cut me real good and took a chunk out of my leg. I'm going to repay the favor."

"I think you're under a spell, Cadence. This isn't like you. I think you and I should just go home."

"Because you're weak," Enora says.

Mira shakes her head. "I don't see a reason to attack the Samhain Witch. She let you and the rest of us go, if you remember, after we came to destroy her hallowed ground. We made her wander and she let us be. There's no proof that what happened to Enora—"

"Well, she differs in opinion, all right, Raven?" Enora says. "Ain't that right, Windstorm?"

"Yes. She attacked her, Mira. We have to stop her."

Mira pulls me away from Enora. We're still within earshot, but I guess she wants to speak with me alone. Then Mira examines my eyes. I turn. I'm getting so tired of people doing that.

"Cadence," Mira says quietly, "you got me and Maddie out of this same dark magic curse. You saved me. I'll never forget that. But now you're going through the same shit I was. This is a curse. There's no rational reason you would ever meet with Enora, especially after she betrayed you with Reardon. With everything she did to Hawthorne, the Billington house, there's no way you'd ever do this. For all I know, this is just another manipulation by her."

"I'm fine, Mira. I agree, I've been cursed. *By the Samhain Witch.* Not her. That's why I'm here."

"I'm not so sure. For all you know—" She points to Enora. "It was her."

"Hey, Windstorm," Enora says impatiently, "Windstorm, I need your help. I can't fight her alone. Are we doing this or not? Don't forget, you owe me for the magic I taught you. That was the deal. Alondra wanted me to teach you. So I did. That's why I showed you my magic spell."

"That spell is nothing, Cadence," Mira says, shaking her head. "Just like the words you spoke with Liam to free him were nothing. It's dark magic, sure, but it doesn't make your soul evil. Only *you* can make yourself evil."

"Enora was attacked, Mira," I say. "Even she's not deranged enough to do that to herself. Who else cursed me if it wasn't the Samhain Witch?"

"Are we doing this or not, Katie?" Enora asks, rubbing her eyes. "Hmm? I don't care if Mira wants to tag along, but I think it's not advisable to stand here till the Samhain Witch decides to go on the offensive. Pretty soon hunters are going to turn into the hunted, if you know what I mean. Hallowed ground gone or not, this is still the bitch's home."

"What do I do?" I ask Enora.

"Follow me," Enora says. Then she turns to Mira. "Joining me and my dear friend Katie, *council member*?"

"Not you. I'm joining Cadence."

"How sweet," says Enora with a fake grin.

"Well, sorry to tell you this," Mira says, "but I already told you guys that I've been up and down this field for hours. She's not here."

"Because you're weak, Raven," Enora says.

Enora pulls out a thin black wand and walks in front of us, deeper into the weed field. She taps the wand on her black grimoire and holds both objects close to her chest. Then she lowers her head, closes her eyes, and says quietly, almost in a whisper, "*Revelare. Revalare. Manifesta Samhain. Manifesta.*"

I jump as the shrill cries of a thousand birds echo among the trees. Then I see hundreds of black shapes fluttering among branches and leaves. Soon they rise and darken the sky. Then they strafe over us. Their caws sound like screams. Groups of hundreds of them break off in different directions.

Enora raises her head. "They'll find her."

"Show off," Mira says.

"You know there really was only ever one true *Raven*, Raven," Enora adds with a smirk.

The black birds spread all over the field. Some walk on the grass, others hover. Many reunite in groups, skimming over branches and leaves again, combing every inch of the grounds.

"Shall we, Katie?" Enora asks, gesturing for me to walk with her farther into the field.

And we're walking. And I'm not sure what's weirder. A thousand birds cawing and flying, or prancing around dead bushes and tree trunks searching for our enemy, or my archenemy and I hiking into the forest clearing together.

This part of the field is empty. The ground is probably more clear of shrubs and stones than the dirt road because this is where the house once stood, yet I don't see even one stone as evidence of the former foundation. Only the clearing. Still, I have to be careful not to step on some of Enora's fluttering black birds.

"You were right, Mira, she's not in the field," Enora says, stopping. "Bitch isn't in the glade." Enora looks around us. Then she smiles, facing the trees. "So, if she's not in the glade... she's in the woods."

"*Resurgo!*" Enora cries.

Again, a thousand caws echo over us. All the birds on the ground flap their wings like crazy. There are so many around me that it brings up a cloud of dust. They rise into the sky, shadowing the sunlight above as if a cloud has formed. Then they regroup and head toward the surrounding forest.

But then... All the black birds plummet straight to the ground. So many fall that I can't dodge all of them. One hits my back hard. Another collides with my arm and rolls onto the ground. On the ground, they flap their wings violently against the dirt and leaves, as if having seizures.

Then they stop dead. It gets super quiet.

I crouch down to look at the one that hit me. Its eyes are closed, and it's lying on its side completely motionless. Dead?

"Holy shit," Mira says with eyes open wide.

Thousands of birds lie lifeless, strewn along the wild grass, leaves, and branches. Only a handful are still twitching.

"Guess they found her," Enora quips with a nervous laugh. "Who's showing off now, Mira?"

"Come to play?" croaks a voice in the air. It's Melanie's voice. I'd recognize that monstrous voice anywhere. "Speak the words again for me, won't you, Cassie-Cassie? It was music to my ears. Damn yourself for truth again? It entertains. Aren't you a witch? Don't you know you're a witch, little ewe? All witches are wicked."

"Close thy soul," I say without control of my voice. I shake my head and cover my mouth, but I can't stop the words coming from my lips. "Turn your back on me, and within feel the great presence of Baphomet through the shadows of darkness."

"That wasn't me, guys," I say, looking all around me.

There's laughter. A thousand voices are laughing among the surrounding trees. It sounds like it's coming from my right. I turn, but I don't see anyone.

"There is nothing left of me," Melanie says, "yet you come to take away my final breath? Why? I have no home. No family. I wander. I drift after that warlock destroyed everything. You didn't destroy my home, Windstorm. I accept my plight if..." She shouts, "*If it means the end of every witch in this world!* Before I go, you three witches will die."

I turn to Mira. Her face is completely frozen, staring at the fields. Enora is violently shaking her head. Then she clutches her head with both hands.

"*Bitch!*" Enora says, shaking and gripping her head. "*Get out of my head!*" Then she shouts, "*Festinare! Festinare!*"

She turns to me, panting. "Why isn't she freezing you, Katie?"

"This is how she stopped the three witches last time," I say, pointing to Mira. "Mira's not moving. She froze all of us last time we attacked."

"I told you a thousand times, Raven is weak," Enora says, rolling her eyes. "I'm carrying red aventurine. What stone are you carrying?"

"Haven't got one." I shrug.

Enora furrows her brow and shakes her head.

Then she extends her wand. She smiles slyly at me.

"Well, now...we know you're here, don't we?" She points the wand toward the trees in every direction. "Where are you, old turd? Hmm? Mud? You want to play? I can play with you, you little piece of shit. Take a bite of my fucking leg? Cut me? Oh, I'm gonna hurt you, I'm gonna hurt you so bad. Come on! Where are you hiding? Show yourself. *Revelare. Revelare.*"

"I never hurt you," Melanie says. "You flew away like cowardly birds."

"*Decipula!*" cries Enora in triumph, turning toward the voice. She waves her wand toward some trees. "*Decipula! Revelare! Revelare!*" She spins around to the right, striking her wand in the air, "*Samhain, Samhain, come forth. Decipula! Venite foras. Come forth and show yourself, filthy savage!*"

Light flashes from Enora's wand and strikes a tree across the grass. Clouds form above. Then a violent wind blows my hair back, nearly tossing me to the ground.

"She's here!" Enora says to me, pointing to a group of trees with her wand and running in that direction. But I don't see anyone. "Hold your grimoire forth, Cadence. I need your energy. Utter the words: *Decipula. Decipula Revelare.*"

"*Decipula!*" I cry, holding *Broomstick* forth. "*Decipula. Decipula Revelare.*"

"*I've trapped you!*" cries Enora, laughing and holding her shaky black wand. "*I got you!*" She runs toward the woods in the direction her wand was pointing. "From whispers of Aiwass to the worship of blessed Choronzon, upon Lucifer, I will you, *be still! Beast!* Six-hundred-and-sixty-six, by the devil's wand, lord Lucifer, by my god, I order the demons from the powers of Astraeus up and down by the inverse Sefirot, unto the depths of Hades, hold this witch to a tree! Move not! Struggle and branches only bind you more. Show yourself, *revelare*, Samhain Witch! *Reveal mud!*"

Mira's awake. She's running behind me now, and I'm running to catch up to Enora.

About twenty yards into the woods, I finally catch something struggling behind branches and leaves. The whole tree is shaking. Some of its branches are falling. As I get closer, I see her. That familiar filthy creature is trapped in branches. Enora seems to be using magic similar to what I once used to trap her in the main field of my campus.

Melanie is naked, coated in mud, squirming on a tree trunk. Thin black serpents slither across her neck, snapping at us. Her white eyes are wide, but that white amid the brown muck doesn't look menacing. For the first time, she looks afraid. Terrified. Then she starts screaming, tugging on the tree branches. It seems like she's in pain.

Enora rushes up to her and slugs her across the face.

"*Attack me, bitch?*" Enora cries, hitting her face again. "*Oh, you're going to play, all right! You're gonna get it good!*"

"Windstorm!" Enora says, looking back, "Windstorm, I have her trapped in the tree. I've weakened her. Finish her. One of us needs to hold her. The other needs to kill her. I have her trapped. Use the dark magic I showed you, close your eyes, and picture her heart. Stop it! Make that infernal life force leave her!"

Don't hurt her.

Alondra? What? Why? This witch tormented all of us, including you and Liam. Enora's right to want her killed. Even Liam wanted her dead.

Help her, don't hurt her, Cadence. Save her, Cadence.

Melanie shakes and jerks in the branches. Then she stares right at me. Her eyes are so white surrounded by all that black and brown filth. She screams. The sight is horrifying. Then her screams echo in the trees. It sounds like hundreds of children suffering.

Enora opens her eyes wide. Her hand holding the wand is shaking as if she's losing her grip on it.

"*Fucking do it, Cadence! Now! What's your deal! Don't wait! Now!*"

"Melanie, why have you been hurting us?" I ask.

"Don't talk to her!"

"I haven't hurt you," Melanie says, struggling. She almost sounds human, almost normal, for the first time. "I've left you alone since you hurt me."

"What about the dark spell you made me use to free Liam? The spell to turn me to evil."

"You already were evil. You're a witch."

"And Enora? What did you expect she'd do after you cut her? You bit her leg?"

"I never hurt Enora."

"Windstorm," Enora says, breathing heavily. "*Windstorm!*" Her hand holding her wand is flopping like crazy. "Fuck! Or Mira! Fuck! Raven! Either of you! Do something! I can't hold her any longer. One of us has to finish her off. Cadence, use the magic I taught you. Do it now! Enter her mind, confuse and finish her!"

"Where's your mother, Melanie?" I ask. "Where's Kathy?"

"Damn you!" shouts Enora. "This isn't twenty questions. You wait much longer and she'll turn this spell around on us!"

"We need to talk to her," I say, shaking my head. "I need to know. Where is Kathy, Melanie?"

"Cadence," Mira shouts. "Enora's right. When Enora's hold is gone, we're the ones who are going to die."

"Exactly!" Enora shouts. "Cast the spell now, Cadence. Remember our deal."

"Where's your mother, Melanie?" I ask again.

"*Who fucking cares!*" Enora screams. "*Get on with it, use my spell and kill her already!*"

"Where's Kathy, Melanie?"

"Fine, you do it, Mira!" Enora shouts.

"Cadence, I'm still a Hawthorne witch," Mira says. "I'll follow your lead. If you want me to hurt Melanie, I can try casting the black magic spell too."

"She's too powerful to be killed by me alone!" Enora says. "And who knows if fucking Raven can even do it! We have to, infernally, work together, Katie! Now cast the black magic spell I taught you! Or try, Mira. Just you two do something!"

"I'll kill her, darling," says a voice behind me.

The wand is flung from Enora's hand and flies through the air. It passes me, nearly striking my face. It is caught by a man, in a dark trench coat and top hat, behind us. Aamon. He's wearing a black suit with chalk all over his face and a black star on his forehead.

Melanie falls from the grasp of the tree. She scrambles along the ground, screaming and shaking her head. "*Abaddon? Abaddon!*" Her shouts echo through the valley. She sounds more like a pained animal than a human. Then I hear children whispering the words. The whispering is so loud that it pains my ears.

There's a loud crack.

Melanie falls on her side. Aamon is holding a smoking pistol.

Melanie stops moving. It falls quiet. All the whispers are gone.

And then...

Aamon starts clapping. We freeze, not due to some magic spell, but because I think all of us are totally freaked out.

"Well done, witches," Aamon says with a wicked grin, still clapping. "Well done. You helped kill the most powerful witch in the world. With the help of my wand, of course."

"Aamon?" asks Enora, kneeling, panting and exhausted. She's struggling to breathe. "I thought you and I were through?"

"In love, but not in magic, darling. We both wanted this witch dead."

He walks over to Enora, helps her to her feet, and presses his lips against hers. And, weirdly, they make out.

Melanie starts squirming in pain on the floor. Aamon takes a peek. Then he extends his gun again and fires at Melanie's back. Bright red pools spring from the witch's thick, muddy naked body.

"Let's go," Aamon says. "But..." He turns and points his black wand at me. "What should we do with these *students*? Shall I kill them too, Panthera?"

"*I never hurt Enora,*" I say. The words come from my lips, but it's not my voice. It's Alondra's.

"What, Cadence?" Enora asks with a chuckle.

"*I never hurt Enora,*" I repeat in Alondra's voice. "Isn't that what Melanie said to Cadence, Raven? But if she didn't hurt you, who did?"

"Very amusing," Aamon says. "You were right. This witch's powers are impressive."

"She has my teacher inside her," Enora says, still staring at me. "But what do you mean, Cadence? What are you saying, *teacher*? What do you mean you never hurt me?"

"Cadence asked why Melanie hurt you, Raven," Alondra answers from my lips, "remember how Melanie answered?" Then I turn to Aamon and point at him. "Bit her? Whipped her? It wasn't the Samhain Witch, was it, oungan? It was you."

"Wait?" Enora asks, spinning around to Aamon. "Wait a second. Is she right? Was it you, Aamon? *Did you fucking land me in the hospital!?*"

Aamon raises his hand. "Of course not. This is a trick. You're going to trust her possession?"

"Yeah," Enora says. "Yeah, I think I am. I told you we were through. I trust Cadence more than I could ever fucking trust you. Is she right or not? I blacked out. I really don't know who attacked me. Last I remember, you and I were partaking in tantra by your altar."

"We've stopped the Samhain Witch. Your job is accomplished."

"It was you, wasn't it?" Enora says with bulging eyes. "You always stumble when you lie. *You scumbag!* You fucking bit a chunk out of my fucking leg, didn't you? Was it tasty, you sick bastard? How dare you sit by my bed in the hospital as I suffer knowing all along that you were the one who cut me!"

"Calm the fuck down," Aamon says. "It was an accident."

"*An accident!* It wasn't an accident. You did it to get to Cadence, didn't you? Accident my ass! You could have just asked for my help to stop her, motherfucker. Maybe I would have agreed."

"*You were afraid of her, Enora! You said you needed to bring Windstorm here to work the spell. You told me I wasn't strong enough!* Well, you used my wand. I brought her to you, bitch, with my magic. Now I'm asking you to shut the fuck up!"

Aamon is still holding his black wand, with his pistol in his other hand. Mira and I are slowly stepping back. But Enora's yelling and screaming in her usual frenzied craziness, ignoring this fact. Then I think it finally dawns on Aamon. He holds his gun sideways and aims it at her head.

"Shut the fuck up, Enora. I warn you. You and I are through? Okay. Fine. You can join their sacrifice then." He takes a bunch of plastic wires from his black coat and waves it at Enora. "Give me your wrists."

"Gonna tie me up and fuck me in the forest now? Cut me up, try some more sex magic in the woods, you sick fucker?"

"I just might if you don't shut the hell up. *Now hand me your wrists!*"

He pushes her and kicks her to the ground. He ties her hands in front of her. Then he approaches Mira and me.

"*Prohibe!*" I cry. "*Prohibe!*"

He laughs.

"Cadence," Mira says, "he just bled Melanie with a bullet. That's a blood sacrifice. He has power in this field now."

He nods, flashing those stupid fangs at me. Then he yanks at my wrists, burning my arms like crazy while binding them with the plastic wire. He throws me to the ground. Mira falls beside me. But he's not done. He takes a rope from a bag behind him and runs it around our waists, tying all of us together around a wide tree trunk.

"I'll be back soon, ladies."

"What are you going to do with us?" I ask.

"Build a bonfire, suck your blood, and take your life force. These grounds are part of an ancient witch curse far older than the Samhain Witch, cultivated by your infamous teacher and Willow. Imagine the power I'll gain from bleeding all four of you."

"It's the sabbath, Cadence," Mira says quietly. "He's going to sacrifice us."

"Aamon," Enora cries, "Aamon, look, you killed the Samhain Witch, that was great. So now just untie me so we can go back to Atlanta together. Forget everything I said."

"You said we were through. I much prefer to bite and bleed you than cast spells. You always said I make a better vampire than a witch. Too stupid to be a warlock? Too dumb to practice hoodoo? Isn't that what you said? Well, we aren't bleeding you for a spirit's hunger. I'm bleeding you for Hecate's power, the magic you taught me, you fucking bitch. Maybe then, after you die, I'll finally become a worthy witch in your eyes."

"You are worthy, Aamon," Enora says. "Those were just silly words. You know I love you."

"I'll be back to grab some tools from the truck to drain all your blood."

23

ENORA'S CAMPFIRE

MY WRISTS AND LOWER BACK ARE ACHING FROM BEING TIED TO Enora and Mira. We're roped to a short tree trunk with Mira on my right and Enora on my left. Our wrists are tied on our laps. There's a nice fire tonight that the asshole Aamon started to help keep us warm. That's nice because it's sundown and getting colder. After he lit the bonfire, he said he still needed to get some ceremonial knives from his car to bleed us. I wish he'd stop talking.

I also wish Enora would stop moving. She won't stop squirming against me. She's so annoying. Which reminds me— isn't it her thing to turn into black birds?

"Enora, why don't you just change into a bird and free us?"

"Aamon enchants the wires," she says, pulling at her wrists. "If I change, the cuff will change with me and remain on my wing. That'd be fine until I change back. When I grow tall, it'll slice off my hand."

"How do you know?" asks Mira.

"He's done it before."

"*Why has he done it before!*" I exclaim.

"Being tied up can be kinky, Katie. We're not all nice and sweet like you."

"What nice friends you have," I reply. "You always seem to hang around the nicest people."

"Well, just because he enchants the ties doesn't mean I can't break free if I slip them off as a human."

Then she gets even crazier, working the ties more intensely with her wrists. She raises her hands and tries to pull the plastic apart with her teeth.

"I'm surprised Bryce hasn't come yet," I say, turning to my other side. "I was sure he and our sisters would be here by now looking for me."

"He was, Cadence," Mira replies morosely. "I saw headlights. Then I saw the shadow of Enora's freak sex partner turn them away."

"What are we going to do?" I ask, heaving a sigh.

"Worst comes to worst, I lose my hand," Enora says. Then she sounds indignant. "Not that you mind. Could be the hand you burned, Windstorm."

Then Enora's back to pulling at the wire, breathing hard, sweating, trying to slip off the band. I start doing it too. I suppose watching her acting desperate spurs me on.

"Aamon is a powerful warlock," Enora says. "That's what attracted me to him. It's not just his looks. He's—"

Melanie interrupts, coughing and wheezing like crazy. She's lying on her side, closer to the fire, next to our three grimoires, a gold chalice, and a skull. I can't believe she's still alive.

"You can't break those ties, guys," Mira says.

"How do you know?" I ask.

"They're police grade. Aamon's a police officer."

"How do you know *that*, Mira?"

"The council knows every witch."

"When Aamon returns," Enora says, "he's going to slice your throat in the same way I did, council member, only there won't be any nice friends to save you this time. He's a cold murderer. When he sniffs blood, he follows through and gives no mercy. Hail Satan."

"Why do you keep saying that?" I ask. "Doesn't it mean you're going to hell?"

"It means I'm free. There are a million gods and goddesses we worship with Hecate. Satan is just our most powerful." Then she's back to lifting her wrists and tugging. "Why do I have to explain this to her, Mira?"

"Katie's Christian," Mira says with a laugh.

"I go to church," I say with a shrug.

I smell a rancid stench. It's like a trash can smell. I realize the stench is coming from the muddy naked body only a few feet away. Melanie's still wheezing and struggling to breathe.

"Too bad we can't trap him," says Enora. "You could have used the magic I taught you, Katie, and messed with his mind instead of muddy-bitch."

"Is that what your spell does?" I ask.

"The spell teaches self-reflection," Mira says. "The blindfold helps witches ignore all elements except themselves. It allows an understanding of the *without* by studying the *within*. It's like the dark magic of scrying, only this dark magic is self-reflection. One who masters it can control other peoples' minds."

"Or make them insane," Enora says with a nod. "I never mastered it."

"Fuck!" She falls back against the trunk, exhausted, panting, finally sitting still. "Motherfucker! He really did it to me this time. Why didn't I ever guess it was him?"

"I feel bad for her," I say.

"You feel bad for who?" Enora remarks. "Me?"

"Melanie."

"*Her?* Her, Cadence? Are you fucking kidding me? Muddy-bitch killed the headmaster, nearly killed Kenosha, and planned to kill us."

"No, Aamon did. In fact, now I see Aamon casted that curse on me. I always suspected him. Like I said, you choose losers as friends."

"Fighting isn't going to help, guys," interjects Mira, "even though I hate Enora more than you, Cadence."

And then we fall silent as if listening to her. I'm sure Enora would have made another snide remark if she weren't so exhausted from trying to free herself. She's just breathing heavily now. Aside from her breathing, it's real quiet. Dark. Out here in the middle of the woods, there's no source of light except our fire. Looking up, I see the stars are out, but there's no moon as it's occluded by clouds. I'd enjoy the stars...if I weren't about to die.

Melanie gasps for air again.

Hmm... I didn't cast Enora's wicked spell to hurt Melanie, but...what if I were to cast a good one instead? Maybe I could heal her with white magic?

"Can you guys stand up and help break me free from this trunk?"

"Probably," Mira says. "Why? The rope around us is probably loose enough if we push up. But what's the difference? He'll be coming back any minute."

"I can roll closer to Melanie."

"Why would you want to be closer to that heap of shit?" Enora asks.

"I can heal her."

"*Heal her!*" asks Enora, laughing. "You want to heal her? You're so crazy. I want to *kill* her, Cadence."

"You're proposing a healing spell?" asks Mira. "That's smart."

"For our archenemy?" Enora objects. "How is that smart, Raven? Weren't we trying to kill her a minute ago?"

"I wasn't trying to kill her," I say. "I was just trying to get her to back off from Hawthorne. But I'd have to touch her to heal her, I think. This is her hallowed ground, Enora. If I can give *her* strength, *she* can take care of Aamon, right? I'm thinking it would be her pleasure to hurt him now. You guys tell me, you're always more knowledgeable about witchcraft than I am."

"But it's not her hallowed ground anymore," Mira says. "You and Liam made her wander. With her hurt, and her magic weakened, I don't know if she'll have the strength."

"You saw her strength before she got hurt. She had plenty more strength than us."

"She'll kill us," Enora says, shaking her head. "It's a stupid idea."

I don't respond. I just lean against the tree and start trying to squirm up to my feet. But... I can't. We're too low to the ground.

"Together," Mira says. "All of us can stand up if we do it together, okay? One, two..."

"Wait," Enora says. "You aren't sure she'll help. Not to mention, Cadence is far from her hallowed ground. She might not be able to muster enough energy to heal her anyway."

"Enora, if you don't edge up this tree, I can't even try."

"She intended to eat me last time we were here, Katie," Enora says. "She had every intention of eating me, if you remember?"

"*Aamon tried to eat you!*"

Enora starts edging up the tree.

But we just fall back against the trunk.

"Try again," Mira says. "Together. Come on guys. Up in one, two..."

We're up and free from the trunk! But then we fall on top of one another and roll away, nearly rolling over the fire.

"Hurry, he'll be back any minute!" I say.

At first, we all move in different directions. At one point the wire tugs hard on my wrists, feeling like my hand's going to snap off. Then we stop and start kicking our bodies together toward the fire. Somehow, we get close enough to Melanie. The stench of her naked body, like a stinky heap of garbage covered in feces—which I've been trying to ignore—is now too close to my nose. I really want to throw up, but there's no time.

I lean close enough to touch her with my shoulder.

"Hurry, Cadence," Enora says. "Finish whatever the hell you have to finish so we can get away from her."

I close my eyes. There's a blinding white light.

My eyes open in a large building with a vaulted ceiling. A large wooden cross hangs above the altar, and a nun is lighting candles on a table covered by a white cloth. No, not a nun. As I look at her profile more closely, I recognize her. It's my dear friend Frida.

I'm sitting on a long wooden bench in Hawthorne Church. All the drapes are open, and through the window I see our forest under a clear azure sky. It's peaceful and quiet.

The last time I had a vision here, Alondra was sitting beside me, and it was like it was *really* Alondra, not just her spirit. At the time, I had summoned her over the threat of fighting Enora. Now, I'd do anything to help Enora fight our mutual enemy. *Oh, what I'd do to feel your presence now, teacher.* But she's not here, Frida is.

"Frida," I say.

Frida doesn't turn. She's lighting another white candle.

"Blessed are you, Windstorm," says Alondra's voice behind me, "under the stars of the night sky and in the candle of Mother Earth."

I turn. On the church door my teacher, in a black cloak, is hanging upside down. Her arms are stretched out, and her eyes are closed.

∼

In front of my face are leaves and dirt. Or is that the beast's awful body? I smell that stench again. Melanie is still wheezing and struggling to breathe.

"Get me my book," I say. "I need my book to finish this."

"There's no time!" cries Enora. "Just try to cast the healing spell and be done with it."

"Not without my book," I say, shaking my head. "I need my grimoire. I need *Broomstick*."

"He's coming!" Mira snaps.

I turn my head as far as I can in Mira's direction and spot him approaching. He's bald without his hat, but his face is still covered in chalk and he's wearing a suit. All three of our books are only a few feet from us, but I doubt we have time to roll together to retrieve them.

"*Venite*," Mira says quietly. "*Venite. Venite foras, liber, Falconsong.*"

Broomstick jerks in the dirt and leaves, edging away from the other books. Then it slides faster along the leaves and dirt toward me. When it is close enough, I pull it close to my chest. I roll closer to Melanie again. She's squirming, still struggling to breathe.

"Melanie, I'm sorry," I say. "Melanie. I'm so sorry."

She starts crying. That makes me feel so sad.

Then I feel pain in my chest. But as awful as that is, it's good because it means her transference is working.

"You guys free yourselves from the tree, huh?" hollers Aamon, coming back. "Where 'ya going? Closer to the fire? Not yet, witches. After I bleed you, don't you worry, I'll cleanse your bodies near the flames."

"Momma," Melanie mutters between tears. "Momma, it hurts. It hurts so bad, Momma." She's not speaking in her wicked, beastly tone; she sounds almost "normal."

"Where's your mom, Melanie?" I whisper. "Where's your momma?"

She shakes her head.

"Where's Kathy, Melanie?"

She shakes her head again.

"What are you doing!" Aamon cries. "Huh? Stay away from that animal!"

Aamon throws his bags down. He's only a few feet away.

"Where, Melanie? Where is she?"

"She left after Winnie was buried, Katie."

"But I've seen her with you."

She starts crying harder than ever. It makes it even harder for her to catch her breath.

"I killed my mother, Cadence."

"*What the hell!?*" Aamon shouts. I feel a sharp stab at my side. Aamon's viciously kicking my back. "*What the fuck are you doing near that filth! I said, get away from her!*"

Melanie groans again. Then she yelps. She was probably kicked by the asshole too.

I cough. Then I gasp for air. I can't breathe! There's a sharp pain as intense as the one in Kenosha's heart, but this is sharp as a knife. It's so hard to breathe! I turn on my side and watch Aamon's boot fly toward me again. I brace for another sharp strike.

"*Bitches!*" cries Aamon. "*What are you up to? Stay away from her! I have a special ritual planned for her.*"

But his body is hurled twenty feet in the air, away from our bonfire.

"*Stay away from her!*" Melanie shouts.

I feel so much pain. I can't turn to see what's going on because every turn stings my chest. But I hear something violently smash into a tree and shake the branches. Then I hear Enora shouting something incomprehensible.

"Cadence?" asks Mira. I don't see her. My eyes are shut tight. "Cadence!"

~

In darkness, in a church lit only by candlelight, I see the vision of Alondra hanging like an upside-down cross on the church door again.

~

My eyes open to Aamon's body being slammed repeatedly against a tree trunk. But...I'm too weak to keep my eyes open... no, I'm in too much pain...

~

I'm kneeling under my teacher in Hawthorne Church again. Alondra is still hanging on the church door.

"What's happened to you, Alondra?"

Her face is decked in goth makeup. There's an upside-down cross penciled on her forehead—with her head upside down, it's right-side up, I suppose. It's applied like black ash used by Christians during Lent.

"What's happened to you, teacher?" I ask again. "Open your eyes. Answer me."

Alondra opens her eyes. They're pearly white.

"Kill the lamia. You learned Enora's spell to cast against her oungan. The council wishes Aamon dead. The Samhain Witch wishes him dead. I want that devil destroyed."

"But what's happened to you, Alondra?"

"I'm not Alondra."

Alondra's body turns right-side up on the door. Her face blurs, like my face once blurred while staring at a mirror. It contorts and alters into my features. I'm staring at myself with my eyes closed, in a black robe, in the shape of a cross. Then my eyes open, pearly white.

"Come back to me, Katie," Frida says behind me.

"Cadence, please come back," says another voice.

I turn and my mother, my *real* mother, Emily, is standing in the aisle. I haven't seen her since she died, but there she is, standing and smiling at me. Behind her is Frida, standing under the large wooden cross. They look worried. This is really my mother. My *real* mother, not evil Alondra.

"Cadence, what's happening to you?" asks Frida.

"I killed my mother."

"Shoot me?" asks Melanie, recovering her vile, monstrous tongue. "Hmm? Try to kill me, wizard?"

She's looking up at Aamon. He's pinned to a tree by its branches.

"*You motherfucker!*" Enora screams. "You tried to kill *me?* Tried to sacrifice and bleed me? Well, how about I—"

"Cadence," Mira says. "Cadence, are you all right?" Mira's still beside me on her knees.

No, I'm not all right. I'm gasping for air on my side, like Melanie was doing before me. Enora is shouting at Aamon, goading Melanie to kill him.

"Cadence!" Mira says. I try to rise to my knees, but my wrists are still tied. "Cadence?"

"*Cut me?*" Enora shouts under Aamon. "*Bite me? Ceremonially bleed me? Maybe she'll eat you, if you're lucky, you prick!*"

Melanie looks at Enora and laughs. Then she turns back to Aamon, squinting her bright, pearly eyes. Melanie runs an index finger along his cheek. Aamon shuts his eyes and his head lurches away in revulsion.

"Is this yours?" Melanie asks, grabbing his pistol from his pocket. "Hmm?" She moves the nozzle to his temple. "I still hurt. You want me to show you what it feels like when you hurt me? Hmm? My friend little Katie knows now."

"Stay away from me, beast!" cries Aamon.

Aamon manages to free a hand and grab her neck. He chokes her and, although Melanie is horrifying to watch, she's half his size. She drops the gun, gasping for air again. Enora grabs Aamon's hand, struggling to pull it from Melanie.

"Use the spell, Cadence!" Enora says. "Quick! If not Melanie, use it on him! Enter his mind, stop his heart from beating, and his death will break his curse! He has to die, or you'll be execrated forever."

Use dark magic against the lamia now, Windstorm.

"No," I say, shaking my head. "No, I won't, Alondra. I told you I don't want to kill her, Enora. Not Melanie or Aamon." I turn to Mira. "What about you, Mira?"

"The council came for you, not him," Mira says, shaking her head. "Whatever you order, I'll follow. I'm a Hawthorne witch."

"*Weak witches!*" shouts Enora. "*He'll kill her and then fucking break the binding!*"

She's right. Melanie seems to be losing the fight. She falls, limp, and the branches binding him are loosening.

Enora gives up fighting and searches the ground. I realize she's searching for his fallen pistol. Then, though her hands are still bound, she lifts the gun with both hands and points it at his head.

"*Dick! Cut me in a sex ceremony!?*"

"Wait! Wait, please, Panthera!" cries Aamon. He lets go of Melanie and she collapses. "No! Wait!"

A gunshot echoes through the forest.

Aamon's head hangs from the tree trunk, blood dripping from a small hole in his forehead.

I hear a thousand whispers. And then children's laughter.

Melanie stands up straight and turns to Enora. The smile on her gray lips looks disturbing. Enora waves the gun at her with shaky hands, but it looks more like self-defense than a threat.

"Are we friends now?" Melanie croaks with a grin. The smile is hideous. "Are we all nice friends?"

"Sure," Enora says. "Sure. We're friends. Just back away from me."

"First little Hassy-Horn helps. Now you. So you may live. *Today.* Now go." She walks right up to Enora and points her finger at Enora's face, drawling, "The *devil* permits it."

Then Melanie roars with laughter in Enora's face. Enora recoils from her breath, just as Aamon was backing away when she held a gun. Then Melanie crouches down on all fours like an animal rushing into the brush and dense trees. But before she disappears, she says, "Thank you, *Kat-hee.*"

I lose sight of her.

But then I hear her scream, *"Now get the hell out of my house!"*

Her last shout echoes through the valley. I jump as a hundred black birds—which I thought were dead, lying on the grass—rise into the air and fly off.

"Don't worry, Melanie," Enora says looking around the trees with a chuckle. "We're leaving."

But Enora searches Aamon's lifeless body. She checks the pockets in his pants and takes out a small pair of scissors. She uses the shears to finally free her wrists of her restraints. Then she walks back to us with Aamon's pistol in her hands. She waves the gun toward us.

"You plan to shoot us?" I ask, lurching back.

Enora smiles wide and then shakes her head. She points the gun at the ground and fires more shots.

"That's six shots. Count them, six, Windstorm. Six, six, six. Six from his six-shooter. I wouldn't want to shoot my dear friend Katie for saving my life." She cuts the plastic restraints from our wrists. "I'm sure we'll all be seeing each other again soon, sisters. Blessed be, Windstorm. Blessed be, Raven."

But Mira and I aren't staying any longer to say goodbye. I'm rushing back to my car, getting the hell away from her. Mira's right behind me. I'm giving Enora, and Melanie—wherever she's hiding—a wide berth, not wanting to be anywhere near this field anymore. Enora sickens me. Was it the spell or desperation that made me trust her before? It seems to have worn off because now I want to stay the fuck away. I hate her.

"Oh, Katie," Enora hollers. "Katie. Thanks for your help. Or thank Alondra."

I stick my middle finger up.

"Don't forget, Katie," she says with a chuckle, "his curse is over, but you still have my dark spell inside you. Don't know if you know this or not—you probably don't—but when a witch imparts her magic, the energy sticks. Not only is there a part of your illustrious teacher inside you, I'm inside you now too."

"I'm sorry, Mira," I say.

"Sorry about what, Cadence?"

"For having you anywhere near her again. Are you staying in town?"

"No, I came straight over by rental car."

"You want to go get something to eat? Bryce and I know a Hardee's we like not too far outside the forest."

"Sure, Cadence," she says. "Glad I could help."

"Thanks for coming."

We reach our cars. Mira heads to her red rental car, takes off her cloak, and gets inside.

"You can just follow me," I holler.

Unfortunately, I see Enora opening the door to her gray SUV in front of us. Her bravado's not fooling anybody. She rushed from the field trying to get the hell away from the Samhain Witch too.

"Are you going to just leave him hanging from a tree?" I holler before jumping into my car.

"The birds can have their way with him," Enora replies with a shrug. "This is the middle of the woods. Anyone within earshot is going to think someone just went hunting and had an accident. Ask our teacher inside you about hunting accidents."

"I'll tell Kenosha all about your fresh murder when I get back."

"I'm sure you will, Cadence," Enora says with a laugh. "Be sure to give Willow my regards. Oh, and Mira, give that whole stupid council my regards. I'm watching them too, by the way. Cordelia and the rest of my sisters miss you all so much. May you all never thirst, Hawthorne witches."

Then the bitch cackles some more, gets in her truck, slams her door, and peels out, spraying rocks and dirt.

I sit behind the wheel of my Jaguar watching Enora drive off. Mira's behind me in her rental car, waiting, but I rest for a moment. My heart is still racing. I'm still breathing heavily. I don't feel pain anymore, but I feel a little sick.

No... I really feel sick. I want to throw up.

I open the door again and vomit. All the trees around me seem to be moving and I swoon. Then I feel something wet in my pants. Did I pee? No... my stomach is aching real bad.

24

FINALLY, I CRY

THE MINUTE I START JIGGLING MY KEYS IN THE FRONT DOOR OF MY home, it is thrown open. It's Bryce standing on the threshold in the dark. He's in a button-down and pants, dressed like a professor about to lecture, but with disheveled hair and deep bags under his eyes. He looks awful. I'm exhausted too. The car read 2:34 a.m. when I parked in front of my house.

"Hi," I say, walking inside.

I parked behind an old blue VW Jetta. That's Maddie's car. And before Bryce starts yelling at me like a complete maniac, Maddie comes rushing from behind him to rescue me. Behind her I see her mom, Aunt Jane. Maddie doesn't let Bryce say a word. She just throws her arms around me.

"We were so worried, babe," Maddie says quietly. "Are you okay?"

I start crying in her arms. I don't know why. I just do. And that makes Maddie cry too. We cry so hard together and, with all the stress, it feels good.

"She died, Maddie."

"Who? Who died?"

"My baby."

"*What!?*" Bryce snaps. His tone is a mix of confusion and rage. Honestly, I feel bad for him. I think a little more of my hijinks is going to really mess up his mind for good.

"What baby, Cadence?" asks Aunt Jane gently.

"I don't know," I say shaking my head. Then I look at Bryce and say, "I don't know for sure. I could be wrong. I just—"

Bryce turns his back on me and rushes down our main hallway.

"What are you talking about, Cadence?" Maddie asks again.

"I think I had a miscarriage. Enora and I were fighting Aamon in Alabama. Aamon is her newest High Wizard. Or was. Well, turns out he's the one who probably cursed me. We stopped him, he died, but—" I brush my tears with the sleeve of my sweater. "I think it's from all the stress over everything that happened. I healed Melanie, but in healing Melanie, I think the stress was just too much for little Chandra."

"Chandra?" asks Maddie again. "Who's Chandra? Katie, I don't understand what you're talking about. And, of all people, why would you heal *Melanie*?"

"I was pregnant, Maddie."

"Pregnant!" Bryce shouts in another room.

I think he's in the dining room, and he's finally completely flipped his lid. The lights are on down the hallway. He was probably grading finals all night. Now his voice was so high-pitched, it sounded like someone I don't even recognize.

"You're pregnant!" He cries again, still in another room. "But you went on this wild goose chase to meet Enora in another state? You drove five hundred miles to meet our archenemy? Then you cast magic, all the while knowing you have our baby inside you? Did you know you were pregnant when you left? Or later? Or is it even ours?"

"Quiet, Bryce!" Maddie hollers back. "Just shut up. God, you're not helping!"

Maddie's in my arms, holding me. Because...I'm just crying. No, we're crying.

"The curse is over," I whisper in her ear.

"Are you sure, babe?" she whispers back.

"Yes," I say with a nod.

"Katie?" asks a voice.

That's a Brazilian accent. An accent I'd recognize anywhere. An accent I've learned to love so much.

I look up and the best thing I've seen in months is shyly standing by the hallway with her hands in her pockets. Seeing her is almost as wonderful as when I saw my mom in my vision in the church. But, for the moment, it just makes more tears. I'm wondering if the curse kept me from crying before, because now I just can't stop. I even got Aunt Jane to cry.

Is crying bad? Maybe crying is done by good people, not evil ones? Maybe it's the bad people who don't cry? Like, only bad people think crying is weak? Maybe it's the opposite of numbness. Maybe all that numbness, all that blackness, is bad? So am I good again?

"I'm so sorry, Frida," I say in a broken voice. She comes over and hugs us too. "I didn't mean all the things I said to you. I so cherish our friendship. But...you don't have to be near me if you don't want to."

"I was wrong, Katie," Frida says, embracing me again. "I'm so sorry too. I was wrong to leave you. I left when you needed me the most. Maddie's right. I want to follow God, but I don't want to lose friends. And with all the darkness, I just know God still loves you and celebrates our love. I love you so much, Cadence."

"I didn't mean all those mean things I said. It was a spell."

"I know," she says with a nod.

Bryce is standing by the dining room in the shadows.

"I...I'm sorry, Bryce."

"We drove all the way to Alabama to look for you," he says.

"All of us, including Frida, returned to Geneva Forest. Enora's henchman tricked us, leading us to some vacant trailer park. When we realized you and Enora weren't there, we raced back, but you were gone."

"Mira and I must have left by the time you returned."

"Mira was there too?" asks Maddie.

"Raven—or, the other Raven—was there, yes," I say with a nod. "Mira's part of the Witch council now. She said she was sent by the council in place of Kenosha. At first, Aamon took us prisoner, but then I healed Melanie. Melanie then trapped Aamon, and Enora shot him. It was Aamon all along, guys. That's why my curse is over. It was never Melanie, or Enora, it was that devil Aamon."

"But what's all this about a baby, babe?" Maddie asks.

I look down. "I don't know. I bled in Alabama after I tested positive yesterday with a pregnancy test."

"You can bleed but still be pregnant," Frida says.

"Really?"

"Sure, Katie," Frida says, flashing her sweet smile, which I love. "My cousin bled when she was pregnant with Elijah. Bleeding happens all the time in the first few months of pregnancy."

"But I was under so much stress in Alabama. I'm so scared."

"You met with Enora knowing you were pregnant?" Bryce snaps, still down the hallway. "That's so irresponsible. You should never have left Hawthorne."

He sounds like a mean old dad again. And what the hell is he talking about? I can't be pregnant and travel to Alabama? Or I can't cast spells with Enora? He sounds cruel. It's like he's the one with a curse now. And I think all my friends and Aunt Jane agree. We're all staring back at him.

Bryce frowns, quickly runs his fingers through his messy hair, and then rushes upstairs alone.

"Cadence," says Aunt Jane, "being away and not knowing

your whereabouts tore Bryce apart. Maddie and I came by at first for him more than you."

"I know all this has been hard on him," I say with a nod. "I know. I'll talk to him."

"Katie, your baby will be fine," Frida says with a smile, touching my shoulder.

"Chandra," I correct her. Then I hug her again. "I hope so, Frida. Oh Frida, I can only hope Chandra will turn out as sweet as you. God willing."

25

DOCTOR MOREY

I really don't ever talk to Bryce. I mean, he drove me to my appointment this morning at a medical clinic in Flintwood. He insisted that he drive because of my "condition." But we don't talk. As if to prove that he's more *responsible* than I am, he even set up an emergency doctor's appointment right away.

Now I'm lying on my back in a green hospital gown staring at an ultrasound screen. Bryce is sitting on a stool beside me, nervously staring at the screen too. On the other side of the exam table is Doctor Morey.

Doctor Morey is a young doctor with long blond hair. She seems really nice. I told her about my bleeding but, like Frida, she reassured me that the baby could still be fine.

"Okay, this is going to be cold, Cadence," Doctor Morey says with a big grin. "The pain has stopped?"

I nod.

She smiles and squeezes some blue goo from a large tube onto a white plastic thingy and touches my belly. It's cold. But that's okay because all my cramping and bleeding has stopped. Then she starts moving the wand around. Lots of white streaks appear on a black-and-white monitor, and I have no idea what we're looking at.

"You said you missed only one period?" the doctor asks.

"I think so."

"Hmm. Looks like about a month and a half."

"Is she okay?" Bryce asks.

"I'm fine, Bryce," I say, rolling my eyes.

"You're not smoking, right?" the doctor asks.

I shake my head.

"And no alcohol."

I bite my lip. "I had a sip of whiskey."

She laughs. "Just a sip, Cadence?"

I nod.

"I want you to start taking prenatal vitamins. Okay? Of course, avoid all alcohol and smoking."

"I'm already taking prenatals."

"What do you mean a month and a half?" Bryce asks.

"Seven weeks, to be exact, by my measurements," she says. She taps the screen with her fingernail. "See this bulge here. That's a head. And down here, you see the baby's butt. That's your baby. We'll take a photo you can take home. And then look here, at that thing pulsing. That's your baby's heartbeat."

"So she's okay?" I ask.

"Your baby looks healthy to me, Cadence. But I don't know if it's a *she*. I can't tell if it's a boy or a girl yet."

"Oh, Bryce," I say, turning to him. "Bryce, our baby girl. It's our baby girl!"

Bryce squeezes my hand tightly. Then he smiles at me for the first time.

"I'm sorry," I say.

"Of course, you'll have to keep watch," the doctor says, pulling her wand away and wiping off the goo. "Miscarriages are still common at this time. If you bleed heavily you need to let us know. But looking at your cervix earlier, Cadence, I didn't see any threatened abortion. You weren't having a miscarriage. Your cervix was closed and healthy. I think it's just that the area is more friable and bleeds more easily at this stage."

"That's what my friend Frida thought."

"Go about your normal activity," she says, wheeling her stool back. "That includes sex. You're not taking any medications, which is perfect. If you get sick, Tylenol only. Okay? Try to avoid cough and congestion meds unless you have to. Benadryl is fine. I'll see you in another month for follow up. Okay? It was nice meeting you two. And congratulations."

Then she looks at us, waiting for questions.

Bryce responds by hugging me tightly. He kisses my cheek.

"Oh, Bryce," I say, looking into his eyes. "I'm so sorry. I love you."

"I love you, Cadence. I love you so much."

26

FINALS

I'm walking down a side aisle handing out the final exam booklets for our metaphysical history class. This isn't the first metaphysical class I've proctored exams in, but it's the last class of the year. A few extra helpers from administration are helping me pass out exams. My hubby, Dr. Wallace, is sitting on the stage with his laptop, already researching topics for next year. He works so hard. You know, I don't think it's just Kenosha that pushes him. Sometimes I think he drives himself. Occasionally he'll look out at the audience for cheaters. But the other helpers and I are really the police.

Bryce looks so stern and quiet up there. He's been a little bit that way with me too. After the doctor's appointment yesterday, our initial joy faded and we went back to that groove of solemnity. What do you expect? I walked out on him on our anniversary dinner. Then I tried to strike the restaurant with a lightning bolt. Remember? We really haven't totally hashed things out. We will.

When all the exams are passed out, I head back onstage. Then I take the small microphone I left on the podium and stand beside Bryce at the center of the stage.

"Okay, everyone," I say, "you all have the rest of the period to submit your answers. Remember, there are two essay questions at the back. If I were you, I'd answer the multiple choice questions first, but leave enough time for your discussion toward the end. Good luck."

But they don't start their exams. There's too much murmuring at the back of the hall.

A woman in a purple and yellow suit is walking down the aisle. She has dark curly hair and dark skin. I recognize her immediately. It's Kenosha! And all three hundred of our students love seeing her.

She walks right up to Bryce and me. She nods at Bryce and then waves to me. Then she reaches out her hand for my small microphone and pins it to her collar.

She clears her throat. Then she can't get a word in, because the hall is crazy with applause.

"Thank you," Kenosha says. "Thank you. Thanks to all of you." Then she nods to Bryce and me. "Dr. Wallace. Mrs. Wallace." She turns to the audience. "Students. This is the last class of the year. That comes with sadness—or joy, for some of you." A few people laugh. "I wanted to visit and say goodbye to everyone who's leaving Hawthorne. This year has been such a struggle for this particular class. You know, as I said at the start of the year, this class means so much to me personally. I came to this university because of Alondra Johansen. This was her class. And I said over and over to your teachers how difficult it is to fill her shoes. I want to thank you professor, Dr. Wallace, and Cadence, Mrs. Wallace, for carrying on this tradition so well."

I nod at her. It's nice and all, but she's still not erasing that letter saying I was canned from my mind.

"The two of you are continuing a great tradition here at Hawthorne University. With Dr. and Mrs. Wallace's help, they have made this class a formidable history course that I'm sure will be respected around the country."

She looks down and everyone falls quiet.

"There have been a lot of challenges this year. A lot. Health challenges. Some bad, like my own." She points to herself. Then she smiles at me again. "Some good."

Does she know?

"We carry on. That's what's important."

She takes a deep breath.

"Before you dig into your exam—which I know many of you want to get over with—I want to give the best students in the class some extra incentive. All students coming back next year who receive an A in this course are invited to come to the Wallaces' house before the start of the new academic year. We are reinstating our special honors program next year. This program will run the entire year, and I would like to invite any of you interested to come. We'll provide more information after this examination. I'm leaving a flyer on the table. All those who excel will receive a special invite by email. It has been a dream of mine to reinstate this program since Dr. Wallace restarted the course. Now it's a dream come true. Unlike the class, which will still be run by Dr. Wallace next year, our special honors program next year will be arranged by our graduate student Cadence Wallace."

She smiles at me.

"That's all," Kenosha says. "Good luck on your final exam. You may now begin." But first they applaud like crazy again.

She hands the microphone back to me and sits down across from Bryce. I turn off the mic and take a seat at the table between Bryce and Kenosha.

"An honors program run by me next year, eh, Dr. Trent?" I ask in a hushed whisper. "So...does that mean I'm not expelled?"

Bryce finally smiles, still staring at his screen.

"I spoke with the committee, Cadence," Kenosha says quietly. "You're back in next year. But don't thank me, thank Dr. Stoferson. He couldn't stop raving about your performance in his class."

"Thanks, Kenosha."

Bryce grabs my hand and squeezes it.

Kenosha turns very serious. "It's been such a hard year, Cadence. I know how hard you've tried. With everything."

"I'm just happy you're feeling better."

"Are you?" she whispers with a smirk. "I was beginning to think you didn't like me."

"Anything's better than Dr. *Brainer*."

"But," she says even more quietly, "you're still on probation. The committee's pretty close to granting Dr. *Brainer's* request. So shape up, 'kay? I have full faith you can do it."

I scan the crowd. Policing the students is one of my jobs as a graduate student, you know. Then, wouldn't you know it, I see a boy trying to look over his shoulder at a girl's test. He's not very good at it. Usually they're much more discreet. I'm really good at catching these bad guys. Maybe I've enough practice watching my klepto best friend?

I wave my palm over the table. The poor kid's test goes flying across the row. Then I stare right at him and slowly shake my head.

"Nice catch, Windstorm," says Kenosha, folding her arms.

"She's the best at it," Bryce says with a chuckle. He's still staring at his screen. "It's like she has an antenna on her head."

The other students in the row hand the kid back his exam papers. Then he looks straight at me again. He quietly puts his papers back on his desk and gets back to work.

"Kenosha," I say quietly. "You invited the students to our house. I never said we'd host. Wasn't that a bit presumptuous?"

"You've been to my house, Cadence. I don't have much room. But we can discuss the logistics later, Windstorm. I wouldn't be getting too happy seeing me back at work. Hawthorne's only going to get tougher next year. I plan on assigning you a lot more work."

But Bryce takes my hand and squeezes it tightly again. Then he kisses my lips.

"Congratulations, you two," Kenosha says, folding her arms. "I think you'll make great parents."

"Hey!" I snap. "How'd you hear about that?" Oops. A few kids look up. That was a bit too loud. Then I ask in a hushed voice, "Bryce, did you tell?"

Bryce shakes his head and just smirks. Then he takes my hand and holds it again. He moves his other hand over his mouse pad, running through some drawings of medieval architecture. I recognize large cathedrals on his computer screen.

"Frida told me," Kenosha says.

I'm staring at that cheater again. So are two volunteers from administration walking down the aisles. The boy's pretty spooked now. He's not going to cheat. All his eyes are doing is staring nervously up at me.

"Hey, Kenosha," I whisper, leaning over again. "Enora said that pregnancy weakens a witch. Is that true?"

"You're powerful enough, Cadence."

THE END

WITCHY ADVENTURES ARE CONTINUED IN SHADOW CAST, BOOK 6, IN THE HAWTHORNE UNIVERSITY WITCH SERIES

THE SERIES

- BROOMSTICK
- WINDSTORM
- THE HAWTHORNE WITCH
- WITCH MIRROR
- RAVENS
- SHADOW CAST
- BELTANE FIRE short story prequel
- SAMHAIN WITCH short story (3.5)
- ALONDRA 20 yr prequel

THE BOXED SETS

- THE HAWTHORNE UNIVERSITY WITCH SERIES
- THE HAWTHORNE UNIVERSITY WITCH SERIES (4-6)
- THE HAWTHORNE UNIVERSITY WITCH HOLIDAY COLLECTION

AND DON'T FORGET THAT THE ENTIRE SERIES IS NOW AVAILABLE ON AUDIO, PERFORMED BY ALEXA ELMY AND PRESTON GEER!

EXCERPT FROM BOOK 6

"CHAPTER 1 - GRIMA" IN SHADOW CAST, BOOK 5 OF THE HAWTHORNE UNIVERSITY WITCH SERIES BY A.L. HAWKE

I'm upstairs, in darkness, standing before floor-to-ceiling windows in my bedroom. I am wearing a long formal dress. My face is for the gods. My hair is straight and perfect. I've got on dark mascara and black lipstick, but my gothic makeup is discreet. A yellow light shines below my feet. It is emanating from my outdoor patio and reflecting off the mist over the surrounding forest and the wild grass in the field below. There are no stars out and the moon is occluded by clouds, but this view is so pretty. I think of all the things I love about Hawthorne—all our trees, our campus, Hilltop Bluff—the view from my bedroom is my absolute favorite. I know it was Alondra's favorite.

I hear laughter. Then the clash of dishes. Whatever's happening below, I think my boisterous BFF, Madison, is guffawing over something. Then I hear "Mrs. Wallace" followed by more guffaws. Okay, that's definitely Maddie, probably teasing me downstairs.

The bedroom brightens as the door opens. "Coming down, Cadence?" asks Bryce at the doorway.

My husband is in his cute navy blue button-down and black

slacks. His short hair is perfectly combed. His face is clean shaven. I shopped for those clothes when we went to downtown Atlanta a few months ago. He looks so professorly. I don't. My long, draping black dress will probably remind the kids downstairs of Morticia Addams. But that's really what's behind this secret meeting downstairs, you know. This isn't a special "honors" program at Hawthorne University, or even a party with faculty. It's a recruitment of witches for Hawthorne Forest.

"Sure, Bryce. I'm coming. I just needed to freshen up a bit more."

"You look great. I was afraid you left for a wandering."

"No," I say with a laugh. "Just...a little nervous, I guess. Not sure why."

"Alondra wanted this, Katie. She always believed in you. Anyway, Maddie and Kenosha are already entertaining everybody."

"Kenosha's saving the day again?"

"Blessed be and let it be, Cadence. Relaaax, everything is going to be fine."

Bryce reaches out for me. I nod and tear my eyes away from our gorgeous view.

My dining room, downstairs, is completely transformed. All these kids look so formal. They're all girls. All genders are invited to the program, but only our "ladies' club" has a special occult practicum, if you know what I mean.

The provost, Dr. Kenosha Trent, is yapping away, in good spirits, at my very long oak table. I'm so glad she looks stronger. She's in a suit with a curly wig, sitting in front of our gorgeous walled window looking out into the forest.

"Cadence," Kenosha says, standing up. "Dr. Wallace."

"Found her," Bryce says with a chuckle. He grabs a napkin, sits down, and drapes it over his lap.

The whole table is totally decked out in this fancy-smancy white tablecloth covered in crystal glasses and shiny silver.

Alondra had some amazing stuff for guests. All the big dishes are in covered trays. Of course, somehow Kenosha finagled the school into footing the bill. I couldn't afford it. I smell those delicious spices, with potatoes and roasted chicken underneath. My sister witches helped arrange the room before the guests arrived, but only a few are here. There are too many guests for my sisters to attend. Every place setting has a crystal glass shaped like a chalice, but most kids are underage and are drinking soda. And there are tons of small lit candles about the table.

I sit at the head of the table, draping my white cloth napkin over my lap. Maddie nods beside me with a reassuring grin.

"Welcome, guys," I say. "Many of you may be wondering why I invited you here to my house."

They're so focused. No...not just focused, nervous. I remember being freaked out when I first arrived at Alondra's antebellum mansion—now my house. Even Alondra herself was intimidating. Maybe I overdid the witchy makeup tonight too?

"Some of you were with us last year in my husband's metaphysical history class. Others just made it here to Hawthorne. Either way, I'm so excited about this new year, and I look forward to meeting all of you. This special program seeks to go deeper into the knowledge of magic and the occult. Many of you might have heard rumors. The program was renowned when Dr. Alondra Johansen was teaching. Well, we don't sacrifice babies or drink human blood, okay?" Some laugh nervously. "But things can get weird." I bite my lip. "Outside of class, we'll meet and talk about magic and try out some real rites. If you're averse to any of this, perhaps finding it against your religion or beliefs, then the program might not be—"

There's a loud thud against my front door followed by incessant rapping.

"I'll see who it is," says Bryce.

"No, Bryce," Maddie says, pushing her chair back. "I'll see who it is. Maybe it's your brother, Katie."

Damie? Hammering on the door?

"Umm...so, the reward for joining will be graduating with high marks from our university. But be warned: we will be practicing real pagan rites. It might make you uncomfortable, so I encourage you to research what you're in for before you sign up. Talk to us."

There's another loud bang followed by a few rings of our doorbell.

"You all won't have to do anything you're not comfortable doing," Kenosha adds. I get it. She's trying to relax them.

"Yeah," I say, "talk to the more experienced among us, like Josie and Jessica or Madison here. Or even Dr. Wallace. We don't bite."

"*You fucking worthless witch! Step aside! I'm not here for a weak magus! I need Windstorm! Where's Windstorm? Where's the Hawthorne Witch!*"

What the hell? That voice makes me feel grima. Do you know what grima is? It's that awful creepy feeling you get when you run your fingernails across a blackboard. It's Cordelia.

"Cadence!" cries Maddie. "Cadence, you might want to come here and—"

"She's there!" cries Cordelia.

"She's in a meeting."

"What meeting? Are you conjuring inside now?"

"Why do you care, Adder? Why not come back another time? *Hey, wait a minute! No! No, no, don't go in there now!*"

Kenosha loses her smile. She quickly throws down her napkin and scoots back her chair. So does Bryce. I rush with them into the hallway.

Cordelia is storming toward us. She's a large broad-shouldered bitch, her face tattooed with black ink, who hung a psychotic friend from my patio once. (Well, we were never sure it was her, but I'm almost positive.) She looks ready to pummel me. She's large enough to suffocate me just by sitting on me. She's wearing a scarlet cloak. With the red cloak and black tattooed face, she looks barbarous. I imagine all those scared girls' faces in my dining room. We can't let them see her.

I block the hallway before she gets closer to the dining room.

"What's this about?" Kenosha demands. "We're in a meeting, Adder."

"Ask her," Cordelia says, gesturing to me. "She's been casting. She knows damn well what it's all about."

"What are you talking about?" I ask.

"You've been casting," Cordelia says with a wicked grin. She looks down on me, as she's about a head taller. "Invoking Alu-s. My sisters have been haunted in their sleep for weeks. Panthera is about ready to go on the offensive, but my circle is afraid of you. I'm not scared of you. It would be my pleasure to go to war with your coven again."

"Why not come back and talk about this later?" asks Bryce.

"Shut up, High Priest. You're as weak as Blackbird."

"Bryce is right," Kenosha says. "If there's something going on with your circle, Adder, let's talk later. Not in front of my students."

"Glad to see you're feeling better," Cordelia says with a smirk, "after this wicked witch nearly killed you. Windstorm hurt you really good, so I hear?"

"I don't know what you're talking about, Cordelia," I snap. "I haven't cast any magic spells against you or your coven!"

"Cadence, keep your voice down," Kenosha warns.

"Last time you guys accused us," snaps Maddie, "it was Enora."

"The nightmares are coming from somewhere," Cordelia replies, shaking her head emphatically. "We know Katie was cursed before, but our oungan was killed by my master. There are not a whole lot of witches with this power left around here. Could be the Samhain Witch, but she wasn't taught dream casting. Cadence was. Unless it's your spell, Willow?"

"*Get out of my house!*" I shout. "*Get the fuck out! Why the hell did you let her inside, Maddie?*"

"Bitch barged in," Maddie says, shrugging.

"Threatening me now? I know I'm on your hallowed ground. I don't care. I told you, I'm not scared of you." She sticks a finger in my chest. "I warn you. As grateful as master's been for your help in Alabama, she's ready for another fight. She wanted me to tell you that we don't cast shield spells. If the dreams don't stop, we're going to fight, and I promise you, witches, we'll bring more than just bad dreams." She looks up and then turns back toward the foyer. "Maybe we'll burn *this* house down this time."

Before I hurl her across the room, she raises her palm with a black tattoo of a backward pentacle. Then she quickly gathers her long red cloak, turns her back on me, and storms out the front door.

The door slams shut.

"Cadence?" Kenosha turns to me, suspicious. "What's this about?"

I quickly shake my head. "I don't know."

"Shit," Maddie says. "I really hate that snake."

"Well," Kenosha says sternly, nodding. She heaves a sigh. "Now we have to explain *spell casting* and *curses* to your guests, Cadence."

"You never know, Dr. Trent," Maddie quips with a nervous laugh. "Maybe all the excitement will really help with the recruitment?"

TO BE CONTINUED IN BOOK 6 OF THE HAWTHORNE
UNIVERSITY WITCH SERIES

ALSO BY A.L. HAWKE

PARANORMAL ROMANCE

- THE HAWTHORNE UNIVERSITY WITCH SERIES (I-III)
- THE HAWTHORNE UNIVERSITY WITCH SERIES (4-6)
- THE HAWTHORNE UNIVERSITY WITCH HOLIDAY COLLECTION

- SHADES
- HAUNTING JOY
- PHANTOM MASQUERADE

- MY EVIL EYE
- THE GUARDIAN
- NECTAR OF AMBROSIA
- CORA

FANTASY: THE AZURE SERIES

- HARMONIA
- CORA: RISE OF THE FALLEN GODDESS
- AZURE BLUE
- CORAL RED
- PRINCESS SOJOURN

SCIENCE FICTION

- CANDY SAVANT SERIES

Books available at https://alhawke.com/books

PARTING WORDS

What did you think of *Ravens*? By placing a book review, you can inform others of your thoughts and help spread the word about my book.

Want more? Periodically I like to send news regarding current or new projects. If you'd like to be privy, I encourage you to sign up to my email newsletter. Your information will remain private and you can cancel any time.

Sign up at www.alhawke.com or scan the following QR code:

ABOUT THE AUTHOR

A.L. Hawke is the author of the bestselling Hawthorne University Witch series. The author lives in Southern California torching the midnight candle over lovers against a backdrop of machines, nymphs, magic, spice and mayhem. A.L. Hawke writes fantasy and romance spanning four thousand years, from pre-civilization to contemporary and beyond.

Visit A.L. Hawke at www.alhawke.com

Email: contact@alhawke.com